Hey Sis -
Thank you for
your support & love.
This is just the beginning!
Plse excuse the misspelling lol!

Acknowledgements

This part of any project is always most difficult because you would love more than anything to list EVERY SINGLE person that has contributed to your success but it is definitely impossible to list all in these few pages. So if there is anyone reading this that I have forgotten, please blame my pre Alzheimer's syndrome and not my heart because without my supporters, none of this would be possible. You know I love you all.

I would like to first off thank the creator. He has definitely picked me to be amongst his great ones and I work every day to never let him down. By just waking me up every day and giving me the abilities to move and do, that makes me great. And it is my job to help others see the greatness in themselves as well.

Next I would like to thank the most important person in the world to me. My mother. Now anyone who knows me knows my mother, even if they've never met her because she is all I talk about. She is my best friend and I live to see her happy. I could really dedicate an entire book to acknowledging the wonders they call Clarissa Eugenia Fields (yup, I put your whole government out there) but I don't have the funding for that yet. *smile* so I will say that my mother is singlehandedly the best thing that has ever happened to me in my life. She is my rock and my sound board. She is the annoying voice that refuses to go away and she is the advice line to all of my questions. Webster hasn't created a word yet to describe what she means to me or what she's done for me so all I'm going to say now is she is the epitome of love! I love you forever and ever mom and I promise to get you some grandkids one day, even if they have four legs, a tail, and their first words are ruff ruff! HA!

This next group of people have helped me with not only this project but have kept their faith in me throughout my many trials and tribulations. My many career changes and explorations. I'd like to thank LaMeica "Danielle" McAdams for being pretty much the only solid female friend I have had for years. (Not to take away from the other female friends I have had.) I know our careers have steered us apart but I can always count on you to be there whenever needed. Love you girl and miss you tremendously. Tell Ben I said what's up with it doe? (I don't know, just sounded like something he could relate to, lol). I'd like to thank Ryan Cauthorn of RJC Travels (I plugged you big homie!!) for being a stand-up guy and waking me up to the realities of how money works, even when I didn't want to listen. You have a keen business sense and you're a genuinely good dude. Any girl would be crazy not to fall for you. I'm proud of you honey. This next person is going to kill me for putting his real name out there but I'd like to thank John "Smiles" Dennis for alllllllllllllll of his patience and dedication with and to me throughout this. I know we haven't always seen eye to eye but you have a special place in my heart. You stayed up late hours listening to my stories and giving me your input. Even though you can be a headache sometimes, I appreciate you more than you know. And I know I'm not the easiest cookie to swallow and I appreciate you always staying level headed with me even when I was being mission impossible. Devon "KoKayn" Reynolds, we have had our ups and downs but all in all you have been a staple in my life for almost eight years now. WOW!! I am so proud of the progress you and Thadd have made in your careers and I know you will only skyrocket higher.

I would like to give a VERY VERY special thanks to Ralph "Big Ralph" MacMurray for designing the Love Sex & Baggage logo! You brought life to my vision. True we always go back and forth but you are an extremely talented artist and you know it. I'd like to thank Chris Maxwell of Liquid Light Images for the amazing cover. Who knew Model Mayhem would bring forth such a great talent? Also, I'd like to thank Patrick "Pac-man" for being my eye candy for the cover; ladies definitely check him out and my AMAZING make up artist, Tasheena Burton for her expert eye and hand. They are NOT ready for you girl!! Thanx to Anthony Tilgham for your continued help and support with getting my name and face out there.

And last but certainly not least, I'd like to just shout out a few people who may have not been there the entire time but have still played an intricate part in the growth and progress of me as an artist and this book; Damon Stubblefield from Fly-ish Apparel; Mel Toliver from Credit Solutions Plus; Zik from Events For Good People; DeJuan from D-Hov Events; Steven Alan Davis; Mike Harding; Jo'Rell the poet; Eric Cire; the faculty and my classmates at The American Academy of Dramatic Arts in NYC; Rich Coleman; my Twitter and Facebook family who retweet/repost my tweets/updates about the Love Sex & Baggage movement; Tennille Patterson; Ricky Tyree from Sirrah Films; and Kory Ray Smith from Visually Ink Lined… As I said, I know I'm probably forgetting a lot of people and someone will hit me up about forgetting their name so just know that I mean well.

Thank you all again for your continued support and I hope you enjoy this book. This is my open heart right here, be gentle. *smile*

Table of Contents

LOVE

*L*ove is Beautiful

"I would like to toast to the most beautiful, talented, and driven wife a man could ever ask for on her Emmy nomination. I am so proud of you, Zahria. You've come so far and have fought so hard and deserve every ounce of recognition that you've been getting and more. I am proud to claim you as mine. And not just cause of your gorgeous smile and big ol' booty either."

"Oh gee honey, you sure know how to sweet talk a girl," I laughed as my husband leaned over and planted a kiss on my cheek.

"Now let's all enjoy the rest of this wonderful dinner and don't drink too much cause we aint driving any of yall home," he playfully mocked.

We were celebrating my Emmy nomination for my talk show. I was more than ecstatic because this whole project had been an uphill battle but one that was paying off tremendously. As I looked around the room, I could truly say that I was blessed to have so many family and friends who support and love me, but most of all, a husband of three wonderful years who had been my rock. Larry and I met on a movie set four years ago when both of us had just started our acting careers; and we hit it off immediately. I know it might be a little pretentious of me to say but he and I were pretty much perfect together. Don't get me wrong, no two people are perfect but I do believe that together, he and I had formed an as close to perfect union as two humans could create. I loved that man with all of my heart and really don't know if I would even be standing in the position I was in had he not been around. I could truly say that in my twenty eight years of living, I had never met someone who made me smile on a continued basis; not to mention that he was a hottie. This girl was blessed; a booming career, a great team behind me and a wonderful, loving, and gorgeous man beside me. Life for me as I knew it was wonderful.

"Hey beautiful, can I have this dance," Larry whispered in my ear, snapping me back to reality.

"Thought you'd never ask."

"Zahria, have I told you lately how much I love you?" he asked into my ear as we slow danced to the soothing jazz music being played by the live band.

"You have, my love. Believe it was five minutes ago."

"Well that's five minutes too long. I want you to know every second of the day how much you are loved by yours truly," he playfully said, pointing to himself. "But seriously," he added, "I am really proud of you Zah and want you to know that we're in this for the long haul. From the moment we met on set, I knew you weren't going to just be any old run of the mill actress. You inspire me to work harder at my craft and at being your husband." He leaned in and kissed me gently on the lips and my knees almost gave in. Even after all this time together, Larry still could make me melt with just a simple kiss on the lips. At 6'3, 210lbs, he was the perfect match to my 5'4 petite frame. I remember walking on the movie set for the first time and seeing him in makeup with no shirt on. Now I've never been one to drool over a shirtless man but it was something about him that made my heart stop. From his big round charcoal eyes to the light freckles on his fair skinned face and the mounds of muscles all over his body; even the full arm of tattoos became appealing to me. It seemed that everything about this man was perfection. And when he spoke, my whole body vibrated from his deep baritone sound. Larry was the kind of man that you had no choice but to do a double take when you passed him on the street. I've always been a woman who could appreciate a dark skinned man but his light complexion did wonders to my soul. And as I got to know him, I found that his heart and mind far surpassed where his looks could ever go. He is the epitome of a true gentleman. He treated me like a queen at all times and made me feel like I was the only thing important in his life. Even when he asked me to marry him, unbeknownst to me, he took my parents out to dinner to get their blessings before proposing to me. And our lovemaking was indescribable. So as you can clearly see, I was truly a happy woman without a care in the world and a wonderful man who assured it stayed that way.

As the night wound down and most of my guests had already left, Larry and I were still celebrating. Never being a heavy drinker, I figured I could indulge just a little that night. Larry always drove when we were together anyway and he only had one drink. Besides, as much as I diet and exercise on a regular basis, this was a needed break from the old rigmarole.

"Lets get going baby. I'm getting a bit tired and we still have some private celebrating to do," Larry said in my ear as he kissed the back of my neck and ran his hand down the side of my thigh.

"Mmmm that sounds perfect" I moaned back as he wrapped his large hands around my waist. I spun around to face him, "are you ok to drive? Not sure if I am. You know I'm a light weight," I chuckled and stumbled a bit

"I got this woman. All you need to worry about is which sexy panties to slip on once we get home."

"Sounds good to me. I have the perfect pair in mind, your favorite; the invisible kind."

"Mmmm. My girl. I knew I married you for a reason. Lets go," he said, giving my butt a little flirtatious tap.

We said our last goodbyes to the lingering guests and walked to the valet to retrieve our car. I hadn't realized how sleepy I was until I snuggled into the passenger seat and Larry started caressing my leg. Although we only had about a thirty minute drive home, I closed my eyes and decided to enjoy a small cat nap because I knew once we got in the house, Larry would pounce all over me and I would need all the rest I could get.

I had just nestled into a good sleep when I heard the tires of the car screech and I jolted out of my slumber just in time to see a tree collide with the front of our car. I don't recall an impact but I do remember hearing my name being screamed over and over.

"ZAHRIA! ZAHRIA! BABY CAN YOU HEAR ME?!! PLEASE ANSWER ME BABY!! I'M SORRY BABY! ANSWER ME PLEASE!"

I finally came to and screamed out in agony as the pain seared through my body. "Larry," I whimpered weakly. "I can't feel my legs. I can't feel my legs."

"It's ok baby. It's ok. Hold my hand," he reached out his bloody hand and grabbed mine. "Help is on the way. It'll be ok. It'll be ok. Just talk to me, Zah," he said through tears. "Zahria?! Zahria?! ZAHRIA PLEASE SAY SOMETHING! Please don't leave me! I'm sorry!"

"Zahria, honey? Can you hear me?" my mother's voice sang in my ears. I couldn't tell whether I was dreaming or if she was really next to me. As my eyes fluttered open, I tried hard to focus on where I was. I heard voices and beeping all around me but still couldn't make out where I was. As my focus became clearer, it became obvious to me why my mother was by my side with the rest of my family.

"It wasn't a dream," I retorted. "What happened," I addressed to no one in particular. "Where's Larry? What happened?" I almost screamed.

"Shh… be calm baby. You have to relax and rest. Larry is fine," my mother assured me.

"What happened mama?!" I addressed her this time. "Something's wrong. Why are you just staring at me like that? Tell me what happened? What happened to us?"

"Zahria McKenzie, you have got to calm down! You will not get well carrying on like this. Now I know you are upset but you must calm down my baby because it isn't healthy."

"Then tell me what happened and where my husband is!"

"You need to rest, I said! You don't need all this now."

"If you don't tell me what happened I am going to get up and find out myself," I attempted to move but felt weird like something was missing.

"Tinkerbell, please calm down," my father said, gripping my shoulder and hand. "You all got into a car accident. Larry fell asleep at the wheel and the car veered off the road. Now he is fine and is heading here now."

"And what about me?" I looked down at myself for the first time and glared at the hallow spot where two legs should have been. "What the" I snatched the covers off of my body before my parents could stop me and almost threw up. "WHAT??!!! WHERE THE FUCK ARE MY LEGS?! WHAT HAPPENED TO MY LEGS?!! WHAT HAPPENED TO MY LEGS?!" I became hysterical and my parents tried to calm me down. "GET OFF OF ME! WHAT HAPPENED TO MY LEGS? WHERE IS MY HUSBAND?! WHY ARE YOU ALL LYING TO ME?! WHERE IS LARRY?!"

"Tinkerbell, please calm down. This is not good for you to carry on in your condition," My father said amidst my cries and screams.

"MY CONDITION?! This can't be real! Please Lord tell me I'm dreaming! This is a nightmare! How can I lose my legs??! Why?!"

"Please baby," my mother said through tears while she rocked me in her arms, "try to calm down."

"Why mama? Why did this happen to me?!" I cried in her arms.

"Shhhhhh," She said, caressing my mangled shoulder length hair. "Only God knows why these things happen, baby. We've been praying for two weeks that He spared your life and He has answered that prayer my child and the rest is still left to be answered. But we are blessed for the favor that He has shown us now."

"Two weeks?! I've been out of it for two weeks? Mama, where is my husband?"

As if on cue, there was a knock at my door and Larry entered the room. My heart seemed to find its regular pattern as I saw that other than a few scratches on his face, he was fine. And upon this revelation, I immediately became aware of the differences in our conditions. I reached for my blankets to cover myself before he could see me. Never in the four years of being with him had I ever felt ashamed of myself in front of him but at that moment I just wanted to disappear from his sight. I couldn't even as much as look in his direction. As he approached the right side of my bed, I immediately turned away. I just couldn't bear looking into his eyes and see any signs of disappointment or shame. He reached out his hand to hold mine but I pulled away.

"They let me go last week and I told them that I'm not leaving your side" he said in the weakest voice I've ever heard emanate from his lips. He reached for me again and as much as it pained me, I pulled away. "Zah baby, please look at me. Look at me. Baby, I'm sorry. I failed you. As your husband, it is my job to protect you and I failed. I love you with every fiber of my being and would give anything to switch places with you right now. Please baby I need you to look at me. Look at me Zahria. Please, I'm sorry," he broke down in tears next to me.

How could he really mean what he said? I was now Cinderella at her darkest hour. I was the swan who was getting her just do. My career was over, my life and everything I've ever known was over. No, he couldn't possibly mean what he said. It's only a matter of time before the guilt subsided and this marriage was amputated as well. So why was I spared?

"I tried my best to make sure the house was in order before you returned because I know how much you always get on me about being tidy," Larry chuckled as he opened the front door to our house.

Although it had only been two weeks since I last saw my house, being wheeled in now made it seem so foreign and strange. Looking up, I glared at my front stairwell and was faced with the reality that I would never again be able to walk up them. Before I could react, Larry was sliding his arms behind my back and under my thighs in an attempt to pick me up.

"What are you doing? Put me down!" I protested while holding onto the chair. "Don't touch me! Stop!"

"Zah baby, I'm just trying to take you upstairs. I know you miss your bed. You've been stuck in the hospital for two weeks. Just want you comfortable baby."

"A little too late for that. I don't want you picking me up like I'm some fucking baby!"

"Well how else will you get up there baby?"

"I don't want to fucking get up there!"

"You can't stay down here forever, Zahria," he pleaded.

"Watch me." I rolled over to our unused living room that we used purely for show. Larry never understood the point of having a room full of furniture that you never intended to use but gave me what I wanted without any contest. As I approached the couch, I reached for the arm and struggled to get out of my chair and onto it. Larry tried to assist but I honestly was not comfortable with being touched by anyone, especially him.

"Don't touch me, I got it!" I snapped at him as he held my right arm so that I could lift myself out of the chair and onto the couch.

"Why won't you let me help you?"

"I don't need your pity."

"I'm not pitying you, I'm loving you Zahria." I scoffed at his blatantly ridiculous comment. "Baby, I know this is hard for us."

"US??!" I yelled at him as he sat on the couch next to me. "There is no US in this situation! Just me! You're free to come and go as you please. You still have a career to build on! You still have your legs! All you walked away with were a few bumps and bruises. You should be so lucky!"

"Please baby, I know you're angry with me. If I could take it all back, I would have never gotten behind that wheel. But I am not lucky. You are my other half and if you are hurt, so am I. We are a unit. Always have been and always will be. I'm not going anywhere, baby. I love you," he said, reaching for my face but I pulled away.

"I said don't touch me."

He took a deep breath and we sat in silence for what seemed like days. I was fine with sitting there forever until I withered away. After a while, he finally spoke. "I'll make some phone calls to get this room turned into our bedroom and have doors put on so that we'll have privacy in the event we have guests."

"No, no one is ever allowed over here, ever! And you have a bedroom, its upstairs."

After another long pause, he added, "I've arraigned for you to have a care giver on hand at all times. I've also had a contractor come in who specializes in renovating houses for people with disabilities and he'll be starting work on fixing everything in about two days so that it's easily accessible for you." And again, he paused before concluding, "The doctors said that the easier things are for you the easier it is to transition through this. And in two weeks, we have to go see him for your follow up and to discuss further surgery and prosthesis options."

"I'm not getting any fucking fake legs!"

"Zahria please baby."

"Just leave me alone Larry! Leave me alone!"

He threw his face into his hands and began to sob and for the life of me I can not explain why I didn't feel sorrow for him or me for that matter. All I felt was emptiness. Like nothing or no one mattered. Not even the man that I once felt meant the world to me. He got up slowly from the couch and wheeled my chair close enough to me and locked the wheels so that I could get back in it, then climbed the stairs with his head buried in his chest. I heard him moving around upstairs and felt a twinge of hate for him as he was to blame for my condition but yet he was free to move about as if nothing ever happened to him. I glanced out the window to my left and saw the sun shining bright and some of the neighborhood kids running, laughing, and enjoying the warm summer afternoon. They were all filled with exuberant energy without a care in the world and unaware of the misery that sat inside our brick exterior. I would give anything to be that young and vibrant again. Even just for the day. Before I was aware, tears were streaming down my face as I became more and more aware of my immediate reality. I hadn't realized it but Larry had been standing in the walkway staring at me with tears in his eyes as well.

"I brought you some blankets and pillows," he said, placing them in the arm chair next to the window. He looked out the window at what I was staring at a few moments ago and immediately lowered his gaze to the floor. "It's not the end of the world, Zah. Your life is not over. I made vows, promises to you that I intend to keep. We will get through this together." He looked over at me and I couldn't help but to look away.

"I just want to go to sleep."

"Ok beautiful."

"Don't call me that!"

He picked the pillow and blanket up and brought them to the couch. He placed the pillow next to me and I laid down and glared at my now bandaged knees where they used to meet the remaining parts of my legs. He covered my body with the blanket and went and sat in the arm chair closest to me. He grabbed the other pillow and put it behind his head and pulled the extra blanket up over his body.

As I closed my eyes and tried to drift off to a place far away from there, I heard him whisper, "I'm right here Zah. I'm not going anywhere. I love you."

The next few weeks were a blur. Just as he promised, Larry had the couch, coffee table, and arm chairs taken out of the living room and a bed, night stand and TV put in their place. The contractor put doors up to give me privacy; which I keep closed at all times. I would hear him all day banging away in the kitchen and bathroom, as he was making the renovations for me to be able to move around easily. Frankly, it was a waste of money because other than the bathroom, I didn't plan on ever going anywhere else in the house. I repeatedly refused to take any calls from my agent, managers, and especially any news reporters who for a week were camped out in front of my house just waiting for one of us to leave so they could grill us with obscene questions about what occurred. And I refused to turn on the television; not because I feared that everyone would still be talking about what happened to me but because after only a month, I feared that everyone wouldn't. My show had already been replaced by another show and the latest buzzworthy celebrity news had sent an overcast cloud over my month old spectacle. Come to think of it, it had been a few days since I'd received a phone call or email from anyone on my team. It's amazing how once you're no longer an asset to someone they just disappear as if you never were in the first place.

Everyday my caregiver, Lena, would come to change my bandages and give me meds. Lucky for me, she cooked and cleaned, so Larry hired her as our live in caregiver. She kind of reminded me of my mother, which I found comfort in a little. Speaking of my mother, my parents were the only people I allowed to see me other than my doctor, Lena, and my husband. They flew to see me every weekend and helped out around the house. My mother kept trying to get me out of the house but we would end up in shouting matches that ended in me saying some hurtful things and her storming out. I have always been known to be a caring and tender woman but I just wasn't caring how my actions or words affected others; even towards my mother who used to be my best friend. I just didn't care anymore about anything, honestly.

"You ready," Larry said, snapping me out of my thoughts. Among all the other turmoil going on around me, my marriage had been the most affected. Larry and I hadn't shared the same bed since before the accident and our conversations were on a need be basis. Every day I would sit and wait for the time to come when he didn't come home. It hadn't happened yet but I knew it would; it was just too early then. I figured he was probably only sticking around to ensure that I didn't press charges, since in fact it was his fault. But I would never do that to him. We both didn't need imprisonment. That's why I wished he would give up the façade and just leave me to my misery. "We're going to be late for your appointment if we don't get going now," he somberly added as he rolled my chair over to my side of the bed, locked the wheels and stepped back from the chair. In spite of my daily rehab appointments, it was still a struggle for me to use only my arms to get in and out of the chair on my own. The doctor stressed the importance that Larry allows me to do it on my own which I was more than happy to oblige. I reached for the chair and maneuvered my body on the bed so that I was directly in front of it with my back facing the seat. Placing both my hands on the arms of the chair behind me, I struggled to lift myself off the bed. Although the wheels were locked, my constant pushing kept forcing the chair to rock and therefore making it harder for me to reach the seat. Larry attempted to help but I shooed him away. Taking a deep breath, I tried again and catapulted myself into the seat; just making it by mere inches. He handed me my throw blanket and I placed it over my lap. Once we were outside, the fresh air hit me like a ton of bricks and I hadn't realized until that moment that it had been weeks since I felt the sun on my skin. My rehab doctor had been making house visits as I refused to leave but I had to visit my surgeon for my follow up and the car ride was what I was dreading the most. Because it was still early morning, most of our neighbors were gone off to work so I didn't have to worry about any nosy eyes watching; especially because we lived in a small cul-de-sac where you can see all of your neighbors' coming and goings. A lot of them had tried to stop by to extend their sorrow but I refused to allow them in so they resorted to dropping flowers and balloons off at the doorstep. Ironically that made my front door looked like a burial site. And in so many ways, it was. As if reading my mind, Larry whispered, "I've been meaning to clean all this up. I will get to it once we get back from your appointment; before I go to my audition."

"Audition?!" I glared at him as he wheeled me to the passenger side of our new BMW X5 Larry bought after the accident.

"Brian got me an audition for the lead role of this new action film."

"Hmmm. Well I see things are all normal in your world. Lucky you."

"What do you want me to do, Zah? Do you want me to give up acting and get a regular job? Is that what you want; because I'll do whatever you want if it'll make you happy again?"

I didn't respond to his ridiculous question. I just felt like punching him in the face for his blatant mockery of me and for showcasing it to the world. As he opened the door, I realized that I would not be able to get into the SUV by myself. I closed my eyes, took a deep breath and said, "I can't get up there by myself."

"You're going to have to let me pick you up."

"NO! Get Lena!" I screamed at him as he bent down in an attempt to pick me up.

"What?! Are you serious?!" The look on his face was indescribable. Almost like someone shot him in the heart, took the bullet out and shot him again. Ask me if I care. "You want to call your caregiver out here JUST so that she can come and pick you up to put you in the car?!! When your HUSBAND is standing right here?! Do you know how ridiculous that sounds and how even more ridiculous that makes me look that my wife is so appalled by my touch that she would rather sit outside of our vehicle until the help can come assist her in getting into our car?!"

"GET HER OR I'M NOT GOING ANYWHERE!"

"Zah you are making a scene," he tried to say more calmly.

"GOOD! Seeing as this'll be the only scene ONE of us will be making for the rest of our lives, MISTER MOVIE STAR!"

"Jesus Zah! How long will you continue to punish me?! You don't think I've punished myself enough?! I'm hitting the bottle more and more everyday. You hate me and I can't stand to bear that burden."

"Well then just leave then! That's what you want to do anyway! You being around is just a constant reminder to me of how good you have it. It's been a month already; your guilty conscience should be free and clear now. The pity party can now end. I see how you look at me now. I know you're disgusted by me. How could you possibly still love a monster like me?!" I said in between streaming tears. He knelt in front of me and attempted to put his hand on my thigh, which I pushed away. "I said don't touch me!"

"Baby, you are not a monster. How could you think that I'm disgusted by you? I love you Zahria. I have loved you almost since the first day we said hello. But if you think that for a minute that I've loved you only cause of your looks, then this marriage, this whole relationship has been built on a lie! Of course I thought you were, ARE, a gorgeous woman but that's not what won my heart. If that were the case, I would have fallen in love with every woman on that movie set. I am your husband, baby. Not some fan that likes what he sees on TV and just wants some arm candy. I am not disgusted by you. If anything, I'm disgusted in myself. But we are a team and TOGETHER we will get through this." He paused and stared at me, pleading with his eyes.

After a moment, I said through sobs, "Get her or I'm not going,"

He stood up slowly and walked back towards the house.

"Here's the last of yo medication, Mrs. Stewart," Lena said to me in her thick Louisiana accent, handing me my pills and a glass of water. I often wonder what made her move out here to LA. Louisiana and Los Angeles are like two completely different worlds.

"For the umpteenth time Ms. Lena, please don't call me that. Call me Zahria, Zahria McKenzie, or Zah. But please do not call me Mrs. Stewart," I snapped back.

"I do apologize. You know I'm getting up there chile an' ney say the first thang to go once you're there is yo mind," she joked.

"Guess I've beat you to the punch then," I replied back.

"Oh child ain't nothing wrong wit yo mind. You just survived a traumatic accident. And ya still healin', physically an mentally. Ain't gon happen ova night. You gotta stop being so hawd on yaself. Somebody wasn't as blessed as you are. God ain't done witcha yet. You gotta family that loves and support you and a husband that I truly believe would lay down an die fo ya. I think instead of you askin' why, you should be askin what? Lawd, what now?"

The knock at the room door interrupted our conversation just in time. "Zah, can I come in please?" Larry said from the other side of the closed door.

"Come in," I sighed.

He opened the door and I had to look away because as much as I hated to admit it, he looked extremely good right then. Which made me even more depressed. His burgundy button up shirt hugged his muscular shoulders and chest perfectly and was rolled up to his elbows to reveal his tattoos. It was tucked neatly into his slacks; which were straight enough to give a peeker just enough hint of what he was packing inside of them. I couldn't quite see what shoes he had on but I don't doubt that they were his favorite Prada shoes with the squared toe. Larry had always been a great dresser. He had the ability to make even basketball shorts and a wife beater look like a tailored suit. I used to rival that ability.

"Lena, do you mind if I speak with my wife in private for a minute," he said, putting his hands in his pocket.

"No problem Mr. Stewart," she said to him, gathering up the remains of my dinner and medicine. "I'll be back to check on ya before goin off to bed," she said to me as she turned and walked out of the room.

Once the door was closed, he said immediately to me, "I got the part, Zahria. My second audition with the director and producers went great and Brian called me on my way back home to tell me that they want me for the part." I didn't respond; just stared at my folded hands in my lap. So he continued, "Filming starts in about a month. They said we should be done in eight." He paused and shifted before continuing. "It's filming in Toronto," he finished. That got my attention and for the first time in almost two months, I looked into his eyes. Well actually, more like seared through his eyes with mine. This was it. The moment that I had been anticipating on happening was finally at hand. Guess he'd finally come to his senses. Guess the guilt phase had faded away and reality was FINALLY starting to take form in his mind. I knew it! But instead of relief that I thought I would feel; anger actually took over. Why would he lie? Creating a story about a movie in Canada? Who does he think I am?! I'm crippled, not retarded! He expected me to believe that all of the sudden, he has to film a movie all the way in fucking Canada? He's no A list or even B lister to be filming in another country!

"What's my name?" I asked seriously.

"What?"

"What's my name?" I repeated

"Zahria," he shrugged.

"Oh because for a second there I thought it was Boo Boo The Fool. If you think for a second that I'm going to believe this bull shit lie that Steven and John probably helped you concoct, then YOU might just want to look into a clown name of your own!" I screamed at him.

"WHAT?! You can't be serious?! You think I'm lying?! Why would I lie about something like that Zahria? That's ridiculous! I told you about this movie a month ago when I had my first audition."

"Yea you did but so what?! That means nothing. Just convenience!"

"That sounds crazy and you know it!"

"So you're calling me crazy now?! Oh, I'll show you crazy!" I screamed as I picked up my glass of water and threw it at him, barely missing the side of his head.

"WHAT THE HELL IS WRONG WITH YOU?!"

"You think that just because you're leaving me that you can just throw insults at me?! Huh? Is that what you're doing?! Well come on Larry! Lay it out there! Tell me how you REALLY feel about me!"

"Leaving you?! I'm not leaving you! And I never called you crazy! I said what you're saying out your mouth is crazy! And now, yes, you're acting crazy too! This movie is paying 500k, which is more than I have ever received for one project. It will help with all of your hospital costs and"

"Oh so this is my fault now?! So you're taking this movie in CANADA because of all of MY hospital costs," I sarcastically spit back at him.

He continued, trying to calm down, "All I'm saying Zah is, since I'm the only one presently working, I have to make sure that I bring in enough income to cover both of us."

"THERE IS NO US!! You are clearly living your life and I'm just existing in mine!"

"THAT'S BECAUSE YOU CHOOSE TO! I have tried over and over to make your life as easy as possible. Have tried to make this as normal a transition as possible but you refuse to let me! You don't know how many nights I sit up in that bed crying myself to sleep! You are my wife, my other half. My better half. And when you are not better, then there's something I'm not doing right as your husband. And you haven't been right for two months and I have tried everything! You won't talk to me, you won't seek counseling, and you won't even leave this fucking room for God's sake! I try to spend time with you but you constantly yell and torment me! And as if that weren't enough, I haven't even touched you in two whole months! And you know how much I need your touch. How much your kisses freeze me in time. How much feeling your skin on mine sends me to another world. But more than any of that, it has been two months since you have said you loved me and the night of the party I told you that five minutes is five minutes to long to go without saying it. You are punishing me for how you THINK I feel towards you when I have NEVER stopped loving you the way that I have always loved you. And I express that to you daily! I don't care if you have no legs or eight fucking legs, I AM NOT GOING ANYWHERE! Why can't you believe that?!" he said as he approached my side of the bed. He reached down to hold my hands and I pulled away; but this time he grabbed them anyway.

"Get off of me! You're hurting me!" I screamed in his face. He was mere centimeters away from my face and for the first time in months, I got a clean whiff of his cologne, "Unforgivable". The scent of him sent chills down my spine and caused me to loosen my pull involuntarily.

"Stop yelling and look at me baby, please."

"No," I whined but didn't pull away. "I'm ugly."

"Says who? You? You've been doped out on meds. You're delusional," he said, smiling at me for the first time. "Stop fighting me baby. When we stood in front of those people and exchanged our OWN written vows, everything I said, I meant. What we have, Zah, no man can take away. Love is the most pure and only sacred thing on this earth and when you really find that in someone else, you cement yourself to it for life. I hate that this has happened to you and I would give every one of my limbs just to get yours back. But God has a plan for us baby. I don't know what it is yet but I'm ready to listen if you are. Maybe before we weren't listening and as crazy as it sounds, maybe He just had to get our attention. I love you girl. So stop trying to get rid of me before I tie myself to the lamp post outside and scream to everyone how much I love you and that I'm not leaving you ever. And I know that'll embarrass the hell outta you but it's not like you could do anything about it. It takes you 3 days to get in your chair alone," he joked as I hit him playfully in the face and tried to suppress a smile that I'd thought I lost. "Ahhh there it is," he said, referring to my lost smile. "Thought she'd never come back. We've been walking around here like the damn Adam's Family."

"I'm sorry, Larry. It's just that"

"Shhhhh. No no, there'll be none of those anymore around here. What's done is done. How about a little less I'm sorry and a lot more I love you," he said as he leaned in and kissed me on the forehead. Just the feel of his lips on my skin made my whole body shutter. He stripped down to his boxer briefs and tried to pull the covers back to get in the bed with me but I resisted. "Let me see you. Zahria, you are beautiful to me no matter what," he said, looking me square in my eyes as he pulled the covers back to reveal my two stumps. He looked down at them and I immediately wished that I could run. He softly kissed me on the lips and then proceeded to kiss each of my wounds. Surprisingly, it felt really good. Not sure if it's because the nerve endings were extra sensitive or if it had just been that long since my husband had kissed me but by the time he fully undressed me, I was moaning and panting like we had already completed the deed. As he entered his place of solace, he whispered in my ear, "I don't think you've ever looked as beautiful as you do right now. Know why?"

"Why?" I moaned back.

"Because I finally see peace in you."

"I love you Larry."

"I love you too Zahria. And that's all that matters."

Love is in the Eye of the Beholder

"I can not believe you are doing this Jennifer," my friend Tamela scolded me as we walked into the Fells Point tattoo parlor.

"Well believe it," I laughed back.

"Your father is going to flip out!"

"All the more reason to do it, don't you think?" It is true what she said; the Honorable Judge Wesley J. Dubois would surely have a heart attack if he knew that I, his darling princess, was getting a God forsaken tattoo; or the devil's branding as he so eloquently puts it. Being apart of such a well to do family as mine; I have often found myself feeling like an outcast. I've always wanted to know what it would be like to be just a normal person, growing up in a middle class family, with middle class problems. My sister and brother have had no problem conforming to the ways of our tight knit community, however; they relish in the perks that come along with being apart of such a snooty, er um, I mean high society community. The Hillside Homes housed the most elite African American families in all of Prince Georges County. From doctors, lawyers, government officials, scientists, and yes, my father. My father is an associate judge for the Maryland Court of Appeals; the Supreme Court of our state and the most respected and feared man in our community. Not that my father was mean spirited or anything but with such power being held in one man's hands, people were just aware of the lines to not cross with him or his family. At twenty four, I was the youngest of three and the apple of my father's eye. Everything I've done in my life thus far had been to please him. I was a cheerleader like he wanted me to be; on every honor roll, like he wanted me to be; went to Howard and barely squeezed out a summa cum laude graduation honor, like he wanted me to; completed law school and got hired at the law firm I interned at even before I graduated; LIKE HE WANTED. But in between all of the accolades that I had acquired to make my father happy, I have found myself feeling empty. Feeling like there is so much more to life than what I've been shown. So in honor of my quest for self discovery, I decided to go where no Dubois had gone before. The tattoo parlor!

"I can not believe I came all the way down here with you. You're just going to do what you want anyway," Tamela said, obviously realizing her defeat in her battle to try and talk me out of getting a tattoo.

"Live a little, Tam," I laughed as I started browsing through the collections of tattoo catalogues hanging on the parlor wall.

"Can I help you two?" a voice said from behind us that made Tamela and I visibly jump.

Growing up in the Prince Georges area, I had come across many gorgeous and clean cut men that any girl would spend days drooling over but the creature that stood in front of me left me breathless. He was tall and slim with skin like caramel. He had on a black Bob Marley T shirt that exposed his fully tattooed arms and neck. His dreadlocks were pulled back into a ponytail and yet they still almost touched his behind. His light colored jeans sagged a little but not obscenely so like many young guys do and they were tattered with holes and paint all over them. He was nothing like I was used to and still I couldn't keep my eyes off of him. When neither of us responded; me from being in awe and Tamela probably from fright, he smiled and revealed the brightest and straightest teeth I would never come to expect on a man of his caliber. And the dimples. Why God would you toy with me by giving this man such beautiful dimples?

"So are you two just going to stand there and gawk at me all day? Cause if so, I can more than gladly put on a show," he teased as he started to put on a strip tease to the reggae music that I hadn't notice was playing.

"Um, sorry," I snapped out of my trance. "I want to get a tattoo today."

"Ok, of what," he said, continuing to torture me with his permanent smile.

"Oh uh, I don't know. I haven't thought that far ahead," I said weakly, trying to pull myself together.

When he came from behind the counter and approached me, my heart started pounding through my throat. What the hell was wrong with me? I was never like this around any man, especially not a man like him. He stopped almost too close for comfort right in front of my face and I got a nose full of his scent, which smelled like a mix between berries, cinnamon, and hair oil. I just wanted to bury my nose in his neck and smell him all night. I've always been a sucker for a man who smells great but this scent was nothing like I had ever smelled before. It was natural yet invigorating. And when he spoke, his breath sent another scent of peppermints through my nostrils to bathe among his other lingering scents.

"And where were you looking to put this tattoo?" he said, giving my body a once over. I normally hate it when anyone stands too close to me, but it was like I was under a spell and couldn't move. I felt like he and I were in a dark tunnel and all I could see was his face.

"Umm," I barely uttered, clearing my throat. "I, I, I'm not sure," I stuttered.

"Well what do you know?" he seductively said, taking a small step closer to me and staring directly into my eyes.

"I know that you're a little too close for comfort!" Tamela interjected.

He chuckled as he stepped back. "Easy now killer," he said addressing her. "I come in peace." He turned and walked over to the catalogue that we were looking through before. "If you don't know what you want, just keep looking through these until you do. I usually don't do walk-ins cause I'm normally booked; especially walk ins who don't know what they want," he smiled back at me, "but it's a slow day, so I'll make the exception." He turned and walked back behind the counter and before disappearing into the back, he said without turning back around, "just holla when you ready gorgeous. My name's Flex."

"Oh my goodness! Can you believe that arrogant prick?!" Tamela tried to whisper and yell at the same time in my ear. "He has some nerve! This is why I can not stand people like him. They have no manners or proper home training. Like loose dogs just roaming the streets, humping everything in sight. And Flex, what kind of person names their child Flex," she continued to rant on, although I had stopped listening long before she began. I was idly flipping through the catalogue as my mind kept recounting what just happened. Secretly hating my friend for interjecting and wondering how far he would have gone. What had come over me? I was not normally this free and loose thinking when it came to men but this one did something to me in five minutes that most have not accomplished in my entire adult life. Wow! Maybe it was just the excitement of the tattoo that had me feeling that way. Yea, that's probably all it was.

"This is it!" I gasped as I stared down a picture of a cherry blossom.

"The cherry blossom? Why?" Tamela said with a puzzled look on her face.

"Why not? It's perfect! It's all about change and appreciating the little things in life that make up the bigger picture! Totally me!"

"Ok, but couldn't you just get your gardener to plant some for you? Do you really need to brand yourself with it?" Tamela said, sounding just like my father.

"It's not the same. Besides, my mother would flip if I told the gardener to plant those horrific looking things in her high quality garden," I said, shaking my head.

"True," she agreed. "Well for as long as we've been friends, I know that once your mind is made up about something, there's no stopping you, so lets just call Rex out here and get this over with."

"Flex. His name is Flex," I corrected her.

"Flex, Rex, what's the difference?"

I shook my head as I walked up to the counter and rang the bell. When Flex reappeared, his dreadlocks were now loose around his face which made him look like a lion, and I suddenly felt a little intimidated. He had a very powerful presence that just drew me in no matter how much I resisted.

"You rang," he playfully sang as he approached the counter where we were standing.

"Yes. I'm ready. I know what I want," I confidently said.

"Do you? Well come here and tell Flex daddy what he can give you," he said reaching out his hand for me to grab hold. Although completely crass, his comment made my mind race at the obvious double meaning. As I grabbed his hand, I heard Tamela scoff behind me but paid her no mind.

"I want cherry blossoms."

After a moment of thought, he said, "Hmm. Now isn't that ironic."

"What is?" I questioned.

"You want cherry blossoms to pop your cherry."

"Ex, excuse me? Pop my what?" I stumbled.

"Your cherry," He repeated proudly. "When you're a virgin and you have sex for the first time, it's called popping your cherry. Well it's the same thing in the tattoo world when you get your first tattoo so it's ironic that you're getting some cherries to help bust your cherry," he laughed at my obvious discomfort.

"You can NOT possibly be this vulgar!" Tamela spewed at him. I glared at her as she obviously had gone too far with her insults and didn't care about offending this man in his own place of business. Although I must admit his last comment did make me feel a bit uneasy, he was still providing me with a service and the last thing I wanted to do was piss off a man who would soon be sticking a needle into my skin.

"Relax Chelsea, it's a joke," he said to her.

"My name is Tamela," she corrected.

"Naw, I'm going to call you Chelsea, like Chelsea Clinton. So prim and proper with your nose stuck in the air" he jabbed back, which I couldn't help but chuckle at how dead on his observation of her was. She on the other hand just rolled her eyes at both of us. "Oh lighten up CC," he continued to tease her, "this is a tattoo shop. All we do is talk shit to one another. Once you walk through those doors, you become subject to any and all comments that may be said. So ladies, if you'll follow me, I'll take you to where all the magic happens." He turned and opened the door to the back and we were immediately met by a completely different atmosphere. The front section of the parlor looked very business like with beige walls, tan carpet, and an art gallery like appeal. The back section; however took on a whole other feel. It was like a cross between a strip club; complete with an actual stripper's pole and stage, and a grunge night club. The walls were painted a very dark burgundy and the music that I overheard earlier was blasting through the large speakers located on the stage behind the band equipment. Even the flooring had changed from the clean and pristine tan carpet to a hardwood that, in this atmosphere, seemed stark and unwelcoming. There were four tattoo booths; three of them occupied by tattooed and pierced men who were all branding their next victims. As if Tam and I had "newbies" slapped on our foreheads, one by one, they all looked up at us from their masterpieces and laughed at the uneasiness that I'm sure was displayed on both of our faces. I immediately regretted coming there and was about to turn and bolt out of the door when Flex grabbed my hand and pulled me into his empty booth. "Don't even think about it, my pretty princess," he chuckled as he sat me down in a chair that resembled a death row's injection table. He leaned in close to my face and whispered, "Don't worry princess; I'll take good care of you. Promise."

"Jennifer. My name is Jennifer Dubois," I whispered to him, although he had already moved away from my face and started gathering his tools.

"Hmm, Ms. Dubois. French."

"Creole," I corrected.

"Well excuse me. So sophisticated. Business like. What are you, a doctor or a lawyer?"

"Umm, a, a lawyer."

"YUP! I knew it! You look like it!"

"And how does one look like a lawyer," I questioned, a little offended at his observation.

"I mean, look at you. You're in a tattoo shop with a silk blouse and pencil skirt on with high heels that say, 'Yes, I may be fine as hell but I mean business so don't try and fuck with me,' except you would never in a million years say that out of your mouth. Your hair is pulled back into a tight bun and you're wearing very little makeup, which indicates to me that you want others to take you serious in your profession and not pay attention to your strikingly beautiful looks. Your pearls are a dead giveaway to your classic style and your demeanor leads me to believe that you come from a background of prestige."

"So, how does all of that allude to me being a lawyer?" I inquired, feeling a bit exposed at his observations. Hating how right he was and wishing I was able to be different.

"It doesn't. I just took a lucky guess at your profession and wanted an excuse to openly stare at your body," he said, trying to suppress a laugh as I tried to cover myself.

"Oh my god!" Tamela said from the other side of his booth. I had almost forgotten that she was there. She obviously had not and wanted to make her presence and discomfort with the whole situation clear.

"Ahh, take it easy, CC," he said to her. "Hey Mike, get this girl a drank! She obviously needs help gliding the stick out." Normally I would have been appalled and offended at someone taking constant jabs at my friend but coming from him and in this environment, I began to see the truth in his words. Oddly enough, I started to loosen up and feel more comfortable with him. He wasn't some monster that Tamela was trying so hard to convince me he was. He was just a man who was comfortable enough in his own skin to say what he felt without fear of judgment or pressure of an expectation. And who was I to judge him? All my life, I have been surrounded by people who cared more about a person's social class status then they did the actual people within those classes. Is a person who has not been afforded the same opportunities as I have any less capable of being a good and sound person? "So, Princess Jennifer, where will we be placing these cherry blossoms?" he asked as he scooted his stool close to me. "Here maybe" he said, lightly rubbing my right arm. Before I could respond, he continued, "Or maybe here," he said as he caressed my neck.

"No, no," I said, clearly flustered, "it must be somewhere discreet."

"Yes because if her father finds out, he'll come here and kill whoever defiled his daughter," Tamela shot back at Flex.

"Oooh. Daddy's little princess is being a bad little girl. I like that. So, Princess Jennifer does have a little badness to her after all."

"I am an adult with a career, I am free to make my own decisions," I defended.

"Well if that's so, why are you trying to hide your decision from daddy," he smirked at me.

"Because she still lives at home and her father has eyes like a hawk," Tamela chimed in before I could part my lips to answer.

"Only because my family is big on tradition and don't believe in allowing us to move out on our own until we're married. I'm the youngest of three and am the only single one left," I explained.

"Which," Tamela tried to continue but I interrupted her remark.

"Which is why," I said glaring at her to let her know that she was beginning to say too much "at twenty four, I still live at home with my parents and therefore can not have my tattoo in a place where they could easily see it."

Smiling, Flex commented, "Well then, I know the perfect place." He stood up and walked to the back of the chair. He pushed a button on the back of the chair and it began to slowly recline back. Once the chair was lying on a complete 180 degree angle, he walked back in front of me and gently pushed me back so that I too was lying in the same manner as the chair. He placed his hand on my lower abdomen and began to trace small circles on it. "I think this is the perfect place for Princess Jennifer to put her cherry blossoms. And I'm sure low rider jeans are nowhere in your wardrobe so daddy wont suspect a thing." He glared into my eyes as if he were waiting for a rebuttal, but when one never crossed my lips, he smiled and went to continue gathering his tools and putting on his gloves.

"I can't watch this," Tamela said, getting up. "I can not believe you are actually about to go through with this. Let alone by such a perverse man. I will be in the car. Call me when you're done." She said as she turned and stormed out. Her attempt at such a grandeur exit caught the attention of the other artists and patrons in the parlor and everyone burst into a roar of laughter. I must admit, it was a bit absurd and I was beginning to get the feeling that that was how I looked to them as well.

"You want to go after her?" Flex asked me, with genuine concern in his voice.

"No, she'll be alright. She's just not used to this much testosterone in one room," I teased, feeling a bit playful, now that the elephant had stormed out of the room.

"And what about you," he asked, pulling my blouse up slightly to reveal my navel. "What are you used to?"

"Me? Not this?" I said, referring to his touch.

"What? Being touched by a man? Don't tell me you're a virgin for REAL?!"

"Shhh! NO! I'm not saying that!" I blushed. "I'm just not used to being talked to as candidly as you are."

"You think I'm being candid? Hmm. I'm just merely making an observation and speaking on it. Its truth through my lenses."

"Yes and that's my point. Where I come from, men aren't as forward as you are to speak to a lady in that manner. They respect a woman's presence."

"*Respect a woman's presence*," he repeated. "So you're saying that a man, who continues to tell you that you're beautiful and calls you a princess and adamantly admires your body, is a man who doesn't respect your presence? I would think that a man who does anything less than that shouldn't call himself a man; in the presence of a woman. Where do you come from, princess, Never Neverland?"

I had no comment, no rebuttal, and no comeback. As much as I hated to admit it to myself, he was right. I mean, really, what had he said to me this whole time that made me so uneasy. He had said the truth. That's all. Being surrounded by men of societal clout my entire life, they always made courting a girl almost like a business transaction; all logic, no feelings or love. And within ten minutes of being in my presence, this man who knew nothing about my family tree, was able to give me something that no one, sadly not even my own father has; he was able to give me appreciation.

The only thing I could find to say was, "No, I'm from Prince Georges County."

"Well that explains it!" he joked. "Now I need you to fold the top of your skirt down a bit so that I can get to the area we're going to tattoo. Don't worry, I wont disrespect your presence by doing anything vile like telling you that you have smooth skin or that most women would kill to have a body like yours," he sarcastically mocked. And as if I could feel anymore embarrassed, he added with a smile, "And that any man would kill ME just to have you laid out on their tattoo chair."

As I rolled my skirt down a little, I caught him staring and tried to suppress a grin. What he had said about me earlier was true, I have tried my whole life for people, especially men, to see passed my looks and see me. I've always felt uncomfortable in the presence of strange men, men I didn't know because I always felt that they only wanted to get me in bed and become one of their conquests. Most of these thoughts were drilled in my head by my father; that any man who focused on my looks for too long upon meeting me, was a man that I needed to stay far away from. I don't believe his intent was to be malicious; he was just trying to protect me but what he didn't count on was my unawareness of how beautiful I really was on the inside AND out and therefore my disbelief of anyone who observed it. And somehow, this man standing before me has managed to open my eyes to all of that.

"You ready," he said, pulling me out of my heavy thoughts.

"As ready as I'll ever be," I sighed and braced myself for the pain.

Forty-five minutes later, he sat up and said, "All done. Wasn't so bad now was it?" I looked down at the redden area that now housed a beautiful tattoo of three tiny cherry blossoms in bloom. I was speechless but in a good way. "Your cherry has now officially been popped and it wasn't even that messy," he winked at me as he applied the ointment and bandaged the area.

"Thank you, Flex." He helped me off the chair and held my hand as we walked out to the front of the parlor where we were greeted by Tamela who apparently had not gone to the car.

"It's about time," she said with much attitude still in her voice.

"I thought you were waiting in the car," I said to her, hardly caring about the steam that was coming out of her ears.

"And leave you alone in here for them to do God knows what with!"

"Yea like suck her blood," Flex playfully said and then burst into an evil villain's laugh that made her jump.

"Relax Tam, he's a professional," I said trying to muffle my laughter.

"It's all fun and games. All fun and games. Can we go now?" she pleaded.

As Flex handed me my receipt he said to me, "Hey princess, I know you're a busy lawyer and all but if you have time during your busy schedule, maybe you might want to come check my band out at the Blue Tree on Friday. We play there every week," he said, handing me a flier. "And yes CC, you can come too."

"I'd rather eat paint chips. But thank you so much for the kind gesture," Tamela spit back at him as she scurried me out the door. "I thought we would never get out of there! The next time you get a crazy idea and want to go exploring; don't." she said as we got into my Range Rover.

I laughed at her comment but couldn't quite promise that I would follow her instruction. Come to think of it, other than some minor paperwork, my Friday was pretty clear.

Over the past couple of months, Flex and I, whose real name is Roy but I've sworn on my life to never call him that, have casually hung out after every one of his shows. I've never been a rap or rock and roll fan but his band, Nevermore, had managed to sync the two and make it appeasing to my ears; and obviously to the ears of many Baltimoreans, as every week they've managed to pack the Fells Point club to full capacity. It's usually a great mixture of rockers and hip hoppers and everyone seemed to always be having a good time. It was a little uneasy for me at first, as I had never been in such an environment but once the band began to play and I saw the enjoyment in everyone, I began to loosen up and enjoy myself as well. Flex was the drummer and although he claims to have never had one lesson in his life, he played like he created the art of percussion. I had really come to admire him. He was incredibly hard working as he tattooed clients all day and practiced with his band all night. He did most of the promoting and handled all of the business side of things for his band. He volunteered as a Big Brother and helped out with community fund raisers in the area. He was well liked and respected by many and not out of fear like with my father, but because he made people laugh and because they're guaranteed a good time when they're around him. He also surprised me with his gentleman like behavior; pulling my chair out for me, opening my car door, and even walking on the outside of the side walk which I've come to take for granted as I am rarely found walking on any side walks long enough for a man to do that for me. Needless to say, there was definitely more to him than what met the eye. Flex was a man with a genuine good heart and doesn't mind sharing it.

"Hey princess," he said to me as he approached me with his drum sticks in his hands. He kissed me on the cheek and tapped me lightly on the rear with his sticks. "Mmm. Bouncy; I like that," he said, referring to my backside. The more we hung out the more comfortable I became with his flirtations. I even found myself being comfortable enough to flirt back. But only just a little; I am still a lady no less.

"Hey you. Great job up there tonight. Was that a new song?" I asked as I've become quite familiar with their play list already.

He flashed a full smile at me, showing off his irresistible dimples, "Yea. As a matter of fact, it is. So you haven't been just sitting here week after week listening to white noise."

I laughed at his comment, "Of course not! I told you, I actually do like your music."

"Good cause I wrote that song."

"Really?!"

"Yes really." He paused before adding, "It's about you."

"Me?"

"Yea you."

"But Keys sang about love in that song," I said, referring to the lead rapper/singer's lyrics.

"Yea and he also referred to feelings he'd never felt before and not being sure of what they were or how to classify them. But willing to find out if she is," he said as he stared directly into my eyes. No trace of laughter or sarcasm could be found in his hazel colored eyes.

"Flex, are you saying that you love me, because if you are,"

"Quiet princess," he said, interrupting me. "I'm not saying I love you. I'm just saying that I've really enjoyed our time together and have grown fond of you. And that I'd like to take you out on a real date, not just keep meeting up here. I know I may not be the kind of man that you're used to and the places that you're used to going may be way above my pay grade but just allow me a chance to spend some real quality time with you and show you more of me. Alone. Without the safety net of the public. I clean up real nice and I promise not to burp or fart at the dinner table, scouts' honor," he joked, holding up three fingers as if he were making a Boys' Scout sign. In the eight weeks that he and I have interacted, it had always been at the Blue Tree. I would come see the band play, stay and talk with him for hours until the club closed or walked around the neighborhood, and then drive back home. My mother was starting to question my obvious change in activity but I would just brush her off and proclaim my right to come and go as I pleased. Lucky for me, my father was presiding over a case, which kept him either in court or in his office all day, so he had been none the wiser. In my mind, I wasn't doing anything out of the ordinary. I was merely going to see a band play and sticking around to chat with the members of the band. True, it was the same member every week and true I was madly attracted to him and had caught some feelings for him slightly; but all of that was simply water under a bridge. No one in my family or circle of friends would see any harm in me appreciating good music. But what he has proposed to me was something totally different. Something much more personal. Something that couldn't be explained as just an appreciation of good music. This was more than that; this was his attempt at a relationship. And as much as I felt in my heart that Flex was a great guy; I just knew he could never be a great guy for me. We were from two different worlds. What could he contribute to my world that I didn't already have?

If I kept repeating this chant to myself, one day I would actually believe it.

.

"I'm sorry Flex," I said as I stood up. "I just don't think that will be possible. A 'you and I' won't be possible."

"What are you afraid of, Jennifer? That you'll actually fall for a dirt bag like me?"

"You're not a dirt bag, Flex. Stop that."

"No, you stop it!" he said standing up. "You've said to me numerous times, no one makes you laugh as much as I do. You've said that you think about me throughout the week and that your Saturday mornings are the worst mornings for you because you know that it'll be a whole week until you'll see me again. Now tell me, has ANY man ever occupied your mental like that? You've told me that you admire me for my heart and my willingness to put myself second to most. You've even expressed to me how any woman would be lucky to have me. So why not you? Why, cause I can't afford you?"

"No, that's not it," I pleaded, as my own thoughts were now being thrown into my face at full force.

"Oh because daddy wouldn't look at his precious little girl the same way anymore, is that it?"

"Flex, please calm down, no that's not what I'm saying" I begged him as I sat back down in my chair, realizing the mistake that I had been making all along. Realizing the real feelings that I had towards this man but the fear of letting my father down was too much to bear. Realizing that living up to what others expected mattered more to me than my own contentment.

"Then what is it princess? If I seem to be the epitome of what a good man is and any woman would want to have me. What's holding you back from making that true for yourself? You say it's not the money or your father, then what? I've come to care tremendously for you. Late night phone calls, texting all day back and forth, I'm ready to check you and all the cards are in place for you to be ready to do the same. If you care for me, I'm sure your family will grow to do so too. You got me open girl, and I'm being man enough to admit it. Just want you to do the same," he said as he kissed me on the tip of my nose. He then put his hand under my chin and tilted my head back so that I could look up into his face. He sat down with his hand still on my chin and said, "Just give me one chance, princess, one chance to prove to you that a grungy dude like me is capable of making a beautiful princess from the other side of the tracks truly happy." He said as he leaned in again and kissed me gently on the lips. He pulled away slightly and for the life of me, I felt like a force had overtaken my body as I leaned into him and kissed him hard. At that moment, I no longer cared about anything else but him. At that moment, I was ready to live, to be happy with him. We stayed tangled for so long, that neither of us heard anyone approaching. It wasn't until she cleared her throat that we realized we had an audience. When I looked up, ready to explain my outlandish behavior, I almost fell out of my chair as my friend Tamela was standing there with her arms folded with the most disgusted look on her face. Flex stood up and playfully said to Tamela, "Oh hey CC, long time no see!"

"What are you doing here, Tam?" I cautiously asked. "How did you know that I was here?"

"Well after the first few disappearing acts you had done, I figured that you just were busy with a major case. But after speaking with Michael, he told me that you were just assisting with one and that you didn't have any major cases coming up. So I decided to follow you and after a few failed attempts, I found you here, in this dump," she said as she looked around the club, showing obvious disgust in the place.

"Hey, you better watch your mouth. This is a respected place of business and the only thing that's a dump around here is your nasty ass attitude, so chill out," Flex said with force.

"Please Flex, don't. Let me talk to her," I said to him, pushing him back down in the seat.

"Oh no, please do get involved, FA-LEX. As a matter of fact, you are the one I came to talk to anyway because it's obvious that my friend here has completely lost her mind and I'm here to help her get it back," she smiled devilishly at him.

"Talk to me about what? She's a grown ass woman who is clearly making her own decisions," Flex said, standing up and wrapping his arm around my waist; which I quickly removed.

"Tam, please," I begged her, "Lets talk outside." I was trying so hard to stay calm but on the inside I was screaming and cursing her out.

"Fine. I can't stand to breathe in this place any longer anyway." As we turned and started for the door, I took a deep breath as I thought that I had averted a catastrophe. Tamela on the other hand was out for blood as she turned and said back to Flex, "Oh and Mr. Flex, is it? The reason she won't date your sorry butt is because she's engaged to be married, to a real man, with a real job. No, correction, a real career. She's just been merely toying with you this whole time because, quite frankly, Jennifer likes to experiment," she snickered as she turned and walked away, this time making the exit she set out to make, leaving me there feeling like my whole life had been shattered into millions of pieces and now I was left to put them back together.

"Is that true, Jennifer? Is what that high siddity bitch just said TRUE?!" he screamed.

"Don't call her that," was all I could muster up the courage to say, avoiding his face.

"Oh but she can come in here and insult me at free will?! You know what; get the fuck outta my face. For real. And take your little stank ass friend with you. I can't believe that I actually thought that a stuck up little girl like you could ever bring herself down to earth long enough to realize that there are real people down here, with real feelings who may not have been afforded the same opportunities as you have but are still solid characters. We're not circus freaks or science projects you can just dispose of at your convenience. We breathe and feel just like you do. Maybe more than you do. You may have money and stature but what you lack is self love and direction. You let what others say dictate who you are and what you do instead of standing on your own two feet and taking that risk of finding it out for yourself. I feel sorry for you because at least I know who I am and love myself enough to not apologize for it," as I fought back tears, he concluded, "I really hope you find whatever it is you're looking for inside yourself before you walk down that aisle because once you say I do, you'll be locked into the person that you are for life." As he walked away and disappeared into the back, I stood there for a few more moments soaking up his words as they continued to haunt me.

Before I turned to walk out, I wrote him a note hoping to explain what my mouth had failed to utter. It read:

My Darling Flex,

The reason I can't date you is because I am engaged to a man that I despise. My father has almost as much as arranged this union and I'm not happy with him, I don't love him. You were the only source of happiness in my life and up until this point I have been in denial about my true feelings for you. There has never been anything in my life that I have ever looked forward to experiencing as much as I did with you. My entire life has been lived for the satisfaction of my family and you were the first thing in my life that was truly for me. I never realized how much hate I had for myself and my family. How much I resented my parents for keeping us so sheltered and closed out from the world. They said it was to protect us from the world but really, it was to keep us from discovering the world and therefore really discovering our true selves. And in this short span of time, you've shown me the rest of the world, in you and therefore I have come to discover me. Come to discover that I'm a fan of the new rap/rock music; that pepperoni pizzas are to die for; and that just a simple walk along the pier can make a girl's heart flutter. For the first time in my life, you've shown me what happiness really felt like. You've shown me what appreciation looked like. You've shown me what gratitude, admiration, selflessness, and most importantly, what being an individual really is. I believe that everything happens for a reason and that it was destined for me to meet you. I now know what I must do in order to explore this seed of life that you have planted in me. I am truly sorry for hurting you and I never meant to lead you on. If I never see you again, I will forever remember the lessons you taught me. I love you Flex and I thank you from the bottom of my renewed spirit for everything you have shown me.

Yours truly,
"Princess" Jennifer Dubois

Love Knows No Boundaries

"How was your vacation, Evelyn?" my mother questioned in my ear.

"I wouldn't call it a vacation as much as a bad marriage detox," I said into the phone.

 I had just gotten back from a month long hiatus after my divorce from my ex husband sent me into a deep depression. Gary was my high school sweetheart and we had two beautiful children together during our almost twenty years of marriage. At one time, he was my everything. Already in college, he waited until I was eighteen to marry me and when he joined the army, I was content with being an army wife for the rest of our days. The first ten years was probably the best years of my life. We traveled all over the world and really genuinely enjoyed being around one another. Often times, people would come up to us and comment on how happy we looked; and truth be told, we were. Five years into our marriage, our first daughter Kennedy was born and she seemed to gel us even more together. She was definitely daddy's little girl and he seemed to worship the ground I walked on just for carrying her. The following five years were even better than the first; he was quickly moving up in the officer ranks and his deployments were being spaced further apart, so we were able to spend more time together as a family. We were like the hallmark family, not perfect, but happy. Then 9/11 happened and it changed everything. They deployed him almost immediately and we were unprepared. They were telling him that instead of his usual three to six month deployments, he would be gone for eighteen months, at the least. As an officer during war time, his demand was great. Being two months pregnant with our second daughter Billie at the time of his deployment, we both were devastatingly saddened. He came back home, ironically on Billie's first birthday and I knew that things were different. Always being a very affectionate man with me, he barely hugged me when he got off the plane. He didn't even as much as acknowledge Billie or even his precious Kennedy who was thrilled to have her daddy back. And for the remainder of our marriage, that's how it was. The war really did some damages to Gary that he refused to face. He refused counseling or medical help. For eight years, he just went through the motions of marriage and could not connect with our children. He began drinking really heavy and started becoming irate and quick tempered. Our happy family was falling apart and I was trying hard to hold on tight to what I knew could once more be.

That was until the military police showed up at my door to inform us that my once lovable, fun filled, jolly, tender, wouldn't hurt a fly husband of eighteen and a half years was being court marshaled for the sexual assault of one of his young female troops. Although he was found guilty of a lesser charge of having sexual relations with someone under his command, I knew that my husband had turned into a monster. Immediately after his trial, I filed for divorce. Even though the girls and

I moved back to New York where I was originally from to start a new life together, I was still a mess mentally and had no idea what I was going to do with my life. I hadn't really worked in almost twenty years and had only volunteered at the local theatres where Gary was stationed. I had been in the performing arts my entire life and before meeting Gary, had planned to go to NYU's Institute of Dramatic Arts. My mother was the director of a small theatre school in the city and after months of unsuccessful job searches, I had been offered the associate director's position at her school. Her only contingency was that I go away for awhile to get my head together. So with some of the money I received from my settlement, I traveled for a month to various places and was able to really find myself again. And now I'm back and ready to make things right for my girls.

"Well you sound better and I'm glad you got something out of it," she said, trying to comfort me.

"I got something from it alright. Sunburn and empty pockets," I joked.

"Well that's what a vacation is all about. The girls missed you."

"Oh and I missed them too mom. I really did. The hardest thing about being away was being away from my girls. Especially with everything they've been through, the last thing they need is for another parent to fly the coop!"

"Nonsense! You have some very smart girls. They understand that you had to take sometime to be by yourself so that you could come back and be their mom again. You were doing them no justice walking around there all gloomy and ho-hum."

"Well, I'm back and ready to move on with my girls and start living again," I said proudly into the receiver.

"That's wonderful dear. They should be coming home soon. Kennedy called and said she was on her way to pick up Billie and I told them to go on home because you should be back once they get there. I barely could finish my sentence before Kennedy started squealing in my ear. Those girls love you honey. That's enough to live for right there."

"You're right mom. That's what I discovered while I was away. No matter what's gone on between Gary and me, the relationship between me and the girls have been wonderful. We have been each other's rocks throughout everything." I said, trying to fight back tears.

"You sure are and I am proud of you for standing tall and strong for them."

I heard Kennedy's loud laughs in the hallway and knew that the mayhem of my children would soon come bursting through the doors. "Mom, that's them now. I will call you later."

"Ok, dear. Before you go; there's a new class that starts on Monday, I will need you there at seven to meet with the faculty and students."

"Sure thing mom," I said just as my two beautiful daughters came running into the apartment, headed straight towards me with smiles as big as the sun plastered on their faces that sadly reminded me of their father.

"Good morning students. Welcome to Rising Star Dramatic Arts Academy. My name is Evelyn Brown and I am the associate director here at the academy. We are excited to have you here and truly hope that you gain a wealth of knowledge and growth here; not only in your careers but in your personal lives as well. You know, I always hear people refer to actors as the 'Great Pretenders' but contrary to this popular belief; acting is the most truthful thing you will ever experience in your life. It requires you to leave yourself completely alone and tap into the truthfulness of the character in the very moment of the situation you're in. Acting is not about thinking but rather doing. The words are given to you; you just gotta do it. And that's what we hope to teach you here at the academy. Dr. Brown has had this school open now for about thirty years and has been offered numerous larger buildings to house it in and has grown a tremendous demand within the theater community from prospective students wanting to learn under her teachings, but she maintains her desire to keep the school at its three hundred student capacity. Why is that? Because she knows the importance of each actor being able to properly learn and grow with individual guidance and mentorship." As I was giving my orientation speech to the new students, my eyes kept wandering over to the back corner where the best distraction I had seen in years was leaning against a bookcase in our small library. He was tall and skinny, almost runway model like. Even from my distance, I could tell that he had these piercing green eyes that seemed to be surveying me. I immediately became self conscious as I looked down at my choice of attire and mentally kicked myself as my business slacks and bouffant silk blouse left everything to be desired. Not to mention I hadn't had a visit to my hair stylist since before I left for my vacation; so needless to say, I was not making a great impression on anyone, let alone this scrumptious man standing about fifteen feet away. I focused on the other staff and students in the room as I finished my speech. When I sat down to let the teachers introduce themselves, I mindlessly looked in his direction only to find him staring directly back at me. I almost fell out of my seat when he smiled at my obvious discomfort. Could he get anymore gorgeous? I quickly prayed that he didn't have some crazy sexy accent. He looked the part. This was New York after all. I was still avoiding his constant gaze when my mother finally got up and spoke. Not being able to take the rising heat that was emanating from my blouse, I excused myself and almost made a mad dash to the ladies room right outside of the library. Once inside, I had to blot my face with a wet paper towel. I was either starting an early menopause, which at thirty seven, was not far fetched; or that eye candy out there was giving me a rush that I hadn't had in over ten years. He had to be foreign. I think they put something in their water just to make them sexy on purpose. I examined myself in the mirror and was mortified by my looks. I looked like a boring school teacher. My hair was in a loose and messy updo and the only makeup that I wore was a very rudely bright red lipstick. I released my hair from the pins and let it fall to my shoulders. I tried to wipe most of the lipstick off of my lips and put some lip balm on that I found in my pocket to give my lips a little more of a moistened look. I stepped back and gave myself a once over and was mildly satisfied with what was reflecting back at me. I couldn't believe I was making a fuss over some stranger across the room. I laughed at my silliness and pinned my hair back into a better version of its original style. I washed my hands and headed back to the library where I'm sure my long winded mother was still chatting up her future graduates. Rushing out of the restroom, I collided into someone standing right outside of the bathroom door. Before I could open my mouth, I looked up into those unforgettable green eyes and almost stumbled to the ground had he not reached out and grabbed me tightly by the waist. We stood in our embrace for a few seconds as I fought to catch my bearing and my words.

Smiling down at me, the beautiful man said to me, "You must be careful, Ms. Brown, these small hallways could really cause serious injuries if you are not careful." British. I knew it.

"Evelyn. Please call me Evelyn," I said, releasing myself from his powerful yet gentle grasp. I stood up and straightened my clothes and almost fell back again as I was able to see him up close. There was no doubt that this man was probably the most gorgeous man I'd ever seen but the problem was this man was no man at all. He was a boy! He couldn't have been any older than eighteen, twenty if I were lucky. I had to be mad to be carrying on like I had. I regained my composure and authoritatively questioned, "What are you doing outside of the ladies bathroom, young man? The men's bathroom is on the other end of the hall. Please don't play around in the hallways. You should be in there listening to the orientation."

He placed his hand on his chest and sincerely said, "My apologies Evelyn." He turned and walked back towards the entrance of the library.

"Ms. Brown! It's Ms. Brown to you!" I screamed after him.

Once he was out of sight, I leaned against the wall to catch my breath. I could still smell his cologne and I closed my eyes and tried to shake the obscene thoughts that were trying to force their way into my mind; thoughts towards a young man who was obviously not a parent but a student. A student that was almost my daughter's age. A student who was off limits in so many ways. Yea, it was DEFINITELY the water.

I had almost forgotten how fun it was to be in a theatre environment; a real theatre environment, not one in the outskirts of Savannah, Georgia where no one really appreciated the craft. Being back in New York made me feel alive and working amongst these young actors made me see what I had missed out on all of those years being married. The past three months had seemed to fly by. Spring break was next week and the students were working on their midterm tests and performances, so we allowed the school to stay open an hour longer in order for them to practice. I was making my rounds for the night before heading home when I saw him. Jacques Wellington was his name and he was a second year student here at the academy, which meant he was graduating this year. I had tried my best over the past few months to keep my distance but being in such a small space, it was virtually impossible. As much as I hated to admit it, the boy made me tingle all over. His eyes always seemed to peer right through me as if he could read my mind and that made me incredibly nervous. He had this demeanor about him that read so sophisticated and at times sensual even though he was only twenty-one; which further convinced me that I needed to take my business elsewhere. So when I spotted him around the corner deep into his scene, I beat myself up for not being able to look away. He had his scene partner in an intense embrace and was mere centimeters away from devouring her mouth with his. She said something to him but it might as well had been Pig Latin because all I could do was focus in on the muscles that were sculpted on his shirtless back. They must have sensed my presence because they both looked up at me simultaneously. He looked annoyed at first as his concentration was clearly broken but once he realized who I was, his face relaxed and he smiled at me.

"Good Evening, Ms. Brown. We were just finishing up here. We shouldn't be much longer. Will that be a bother?" he asked in his deep British accent, still holding onto his partner as I tried hard not to imagine that it were me.

"No, no, Jacques. It won't," I said, clearing my throat. "Carry on you two. Don't let me distract you. I was just observing to see how things were coming along with our seniors." I clearly used my authority to escape the awkwardness that was lingering in the air. Even his partner relaxed once I said that and regained her character so they could continue on with the scene. When the two kissed, a part of me that had been dormant for ten years seemed to awaken and take notice. It took notice to how he caressed her back, to how he seemed to know the right amount of pressure to apply to her lips and as they slid down to the floor, how he lightly ran his fingers up her thigh. When she stopped the kiss to say her last line which ended the scene, I had to clear my throat again as that certain something had fully awaken and was flowing in between my legs. I hadn't been this sexually aroused in a very long time and had grown accustomed to it but seeing this young man in action, made me feel a sensation that I never thought I would again. I had only been with one man in my entire life and even though he was no longer in my life, I still felt tied to him sexually.

"Sorry, Ms. Brown," the girl said to me, getting up from the floor with Jacques' assistance.

"No need to be, Shian. This is acting school. If you can't let it go here in front of one, you won't be able to let it go in front of many. An audience of one will be your hardest audience to work in front of. Auditors will give you the creeps faster than a packed house," I reassured her.

"You're right. I just gotta get out of my head sometimes. Well I actually gotta get going. Are we still practicing tomorrow at my apartment, Jacques?"

"Yes. I will call you to confirm," he said, handing her bag to her.

"Thanks Jacques, see you tomorrow. Have a good night, Ms. Brown," she said as she disappeared into the stairwell.

"Good job, Jacques. Keep up the good work. Make sure you close up and turn out the lights before leaving as you're the last one up here," I said as I turned and tried to run down the steps and away from him.

"Wait," he said, grabbing my hand. I turned to look at him, a bit surprised at his forwardness. "My apologies, Ms. Brown but I can't help but to notice that you are always here at school. You are here more than your mother and she's the director. A life full of work is no life at all, is it not?"

Taken aback from his direct words, I struggled to find my words at first. "I think that is none of your business Mr. Wellington," I said, snatching my hand back from him but not moving. It was like I was under his spell and I was finding it harder and harder to keep up with the antidote.

"Pardon my assumption but you are a single woman, aren't you, Ms. Brown?"

"I do not understand what any of this has to do with school or you?" My heart seemed to be beating in my throat as I wondered what in the world he was getting at.

"It's just that, and again please pardon me; I think you are a beautiful woman who should be taken care of by a man who can appreciate your strength and beauty. There's no way I would let a beautiful woman such as yourself just float on by and not do anything about it. That is, if I had the opportunity to do something about it, of course," he said, staring directly into my eyes; making his message clear. I chuckled at him to hide what I really felt. I really felt like taking him right then and there on the carpeted floor.

"You are being totally inappropriate young man and I have every right to write you up," I snapped at him.

"Again, my deepest apologies, Ms. Brown, as it is not my intentions to offend or over step boundaries; I was simply commenting on what I have observed since I first laid eyes on you."

"Well, I suggest you gather your bearings and things and go on home before you step on something that you can't get your foot out of."

"Yes ma'am. You have a wonderful night and again I sincerely apologize if I offended you," he said as he picked up his things and headed for the stairs with his head hung low in clear embarrassment.

It was not my intention to be so mean but his comment took me by total surprise. Partially because I wasn't aware how transparent I was that someone whom I had never had one personal conversation with could see through me like that but mainly because I was intrigued by his candid admiration and attraction towards me. How could this be happening? Maybe it was still the intensity of his scene that had him feeling so expressive and bold. I'm sure that's all it was. Sometimes it's difficult for actors to cross back into reality from a scene. So maybe that's all it was. No need to get all bent out of shape and start stressing. He's just a young hormonal man who had just finished a steamy scene and he was still on high from it. So this kind of behavior is to be expected. Right?

As I approached my doorstep, I had almost had myself convinced that that was all it was. By the time I had laid down in the bed, I had all soon etched in my mind that this was just an isolated incident that would never happen again.

"Ms. Brown, there is a student here to see you," the office secretary buzzed over my intercom. "Jacques Wellington."

"Send him in," I responded back.

It had been a few days since my encounter with Jacques and I had tried my best to steer clear of him. Seems he had other intentions. I quickly checked my reflection in the mirror to be sure everything was in place and immediately kicked myself for caring.

"He's your student, Ev," I said to myself as I heard the door knob turning. "And he's a child," I whispered as he appeared in the doorway looking dapper in his tailor made suit. The seniors were having a sit down dinner with a top agent tonight and they were instructed to look their best. His usual curly locks were gelled back away from his face, which made his eyes pop out even more past his thick brows. His usual scruffy five o' clock shadow had been cleanly shaven off and his baby face looked even more juvenile now. But I couldn't deny how sexy he looked. In spite of his youthfulness, he exuded confidence and an appeal that made him a staple of attraction for most of the girls at the academy. I've even over heard some of the female faculty whispering about him. He was the kind of man that caught the eye of every woman he passed. No matter their age.

"What can I do for you, Mr. Wellington?" I tried to use the most professional voice I could muster.

"I was about to head out to the dinner and I wanted to give you this before I go," he said, handing me a ticket. "It's a ticket to the opening night of my play in The Village. I would be terribly honored if you could attend." He stared at me as if he was waiting for a response but I just sat there staring at the ticket. I couldn't quite understand why he was inviting me. I had overheard him mentioning his play a few months ago with one of the teachers, so maybe he had invited a few of us.

"Oh, thank you Jacques. We wouldn't miss showing our support for you guys."

"We?"

"The faculty."

"No, Ms. Brown. You are the only one I have invited on opening night. Everyone else has been invited to come the next night," he said with a straight face, so I knew he was not kidding.

"I don't understand. Why me?" I asked, having a pretty good idea already of the answer.

"Just say you'll come."

"Well, of course, Jacques, I support all of you…"

"Good," he said, cutting my words off. "See you on Saturday," he said as he turned and left before I could get in another protest.

Oh boy.

Normally the days seemed to crawl by but the past three days have been a blur. Almost like some cosmic force had sped up time just so that Saturday night would hurry and get here. My cab pulled up to the front of the theatre and you would have thought that this was some hit Broadway show, as many people were lined up outside to get in. This play was being considered an Off-Broadway play due to the number of seats the theatre housed and would definitely shine a major spotlight on

Jacques if he did well, as he had a major role in the play. I had no doubt in my mind that he would do an excellent job; he was indeed one of our top performing students and really impressed the agent at the senior dinner. This kid seemed to never go wrong; which baffled me as to why he was showing a special interest in me, of all people. He could have any woman or girl he wanted, why aim your sights at me?

He received a standing ovation at the end of his performance, which he rightfully deserved. The kid not only had good looks, he had talent. I wanted to congratulate him on a job well done but he had a lot of people around him doing the same. I was just about to walk out of the lobby to hail a taxi when I felt someone grab my hand.

"So I hand deliver a personal invite to you and you leave without as much as a thank you?" he said into my ear from behind me.

"Thank you," I said without turning around to face him. Because of the amount of people congregating in the lobby, we were forced to stand close to one another. So close that I could feel his breath on the back of my neck when he spoke.

"Where are you going," he leaned in closer to me.

This time I turned to face him. "What do you want from me young man?" I asked feeling a little bold.

"To get to know you, young woman," he teased back and I couldn't help but to chuckle.

"But it's inappropriate to. And even if it weren't you're a baby."

"Well, I graduate in less than a month and the last I checked, I have been properly toilet trained for years. So now that we've gotten those out of the way, have a drink with me. Let's celebrate." Without waiting for a reply, he took me by the hand and led me outside to hail a cab. I'm not really sure what came over me but I decided to go along with him. It's just one drink. What harm would that cause?

We arrived at this really plush lounge and I immediately regretted my decision. Everyone was young and hip and were all dancing and singing to the music which I had never even heard before. All the girls were scantily clad in miniskirts and barely there tops and I felt like someone's grandma in my floor length dress. I thought my spaghetti straps and silk material was risky but these girls made me feel like I had on a housecoat.

"I shouldn't be here," I yelled to him over the music.

"Relax, darling," he said, caressing my hand.

"Look at these women. Look at how they're dressed and look at how I'm dressed. I could never compete with that!"

"You're right! You couldn't. But who would want to compete with a woman who chooses to look like a hooker? You look elegant; they should be worried about you," he said smiling as he lifted my hand to his mouth and kissed it. My breath got caught in my throat for a second. What was I doing with this boy? My mother would kill me.

He ordered our drinks and escorted us over to the white leather plush couches in the corner. He stared at me without saying a word and I became increasingly self-conscious. I instinctively crossed my arms over my chest but he reached out and grabbed my hand and held it into his. This part of the lounge was not as noisy so conversation was possible.

"You're so beautiful to me," he said, staring into my eyes.

"What the hell am I doing here?"

"If you want to go, just go," he huffed as he released my hand from his.

"I'm not trying to offend you Jacques; you just have to understand my position."

"I'm not asking for your hand in marriage, Ms. Brown…"

"Please, don't call me that here."

"Evelyn, I'm just asking for you to celebrate the night with me. We won't do anything that you don't want to."

"Fine. Tell me something about yourself, Jacques." And for the next two hours that's what we both did. He told me about being raised in an interracial household in Britain and how he was constantly teased and bullied in school because of it and how his time in America has really shown him a whole new side of himself that he never knew existed. He was never considered sexy or attractive back home but since being in America for the past two years, he has really embraced his looks. We talked about his family more and his future goals. In spite of the age difference, it seemed we both were at a transitional period in our lives; trying to rediscover who we were in the world. We had a lot more in common than I thought we would. After a few more drinks, I opened up about my divorce and my girls. He didn't judge and seemed to sincerely listen and comment when appropriate. By the end of the night, we were cracking up about the funny things that have gone on at school over the past semester.

"Looks like we've closed the lounge," he said as we looked around to see that they'd turned on the lights and people were starting to find their way towards the exits.

"Guess so," I said, feeling a little buzzed. I tried to stand up but tumbled back into his lap.

"Looks like you've had enough, my darling. Let's get you home," he said as he kissed me lightly on the forehead and helped me to my feet. Once outside, he hailed a cab and helped me inside. He paid the cabbie for the fair in advance and wished me a good night. I arrived home to an empty apartment; Billie was staying over a friend's house and Kennedy was visiting some friends in Georgia for her spring break vacation. Thoughts of Jacques started creeping into my mind and I wanted to feel his lips on mine. Part of my heart sunk when he didn't join me in the cab but it seemed to turn me on more that he didn't. I hopped in the shower to try and shake the feeling but the shower just made things worse. I stepped out of the shower and wrapped my body in a towel. Still dripping water from my body, I pulled out my laptop and pulled up the student records file that I had saved on my hard drive. I couldn't believe what I was doing. I didn't know how he would react to me getting his phone number from his student file without his permission. But before I knew it, I was dialing his number and listening to the line ring.

"Hello?" his voice questioned on the other end. I hesitated to respond at first as I had no idea what to say. "Hello?" he repeated, a little agitated.

"Yes, hello. May I speak with Jacques Wellington, please?" I kicked myself at my attempt to sound formal at 3 o' clock in the morning. This obviously was not about his grades in school.

"This is he, may I help you?"

"This is Ms. Brown. Evelyn," I corrected myself.

"Oh, hi Evelyn. Did you make it home alright?"

"Yes, Jacques, I did. That is why I was calling. I wanted to thank you for tonight and to let you know that I had made it in just fine."

"Well good. I was worried about you making it there. I didn't have your number and with next week being spring break and all, I wouldn't have a way of knowing whether you were ok for a whole week but I see you did. But how did you get my number?"

Feeling dumbfounded, I stuttered, "Oh, I um, I have all the students' records. I didn't mean to intrude; I just wanted to let you know my whereabouts so you wouldn't worry."

"So I wouldn't worry, huh?" he chuckled. "Why thank you, darling. What are you doing now?"

"I just stepped out of the shower and was about to head to bed," I said subtly teasing.

"The shower, eh? Sounds nice." He said in a low tone. The silence that followed spoke volumes. "What's your address?" I told him without hesitation. I made a mad dash around my apartment trying to tidy things up before he arrived. I changed my sheets and showered again just as he rang the doorbell. Slipping into my silk nightgown, I buzzed him up. I couldn't believe what I was about to do. I had never been with any other man besides my ex-husband and that was YEARS ago. And of all the men in the world to pick to be with, I had to pick one of the most forbidden. He lightly tapped on the front door and as I opened it, he grabbed me gently by the face and kissed me the way he had the girl at school in the hallway. His tongue was warm and pleasant. It didn't over invade my mouth like my ex-husband's used to. His smell was wonderful and intoxicating and I was becoming overwhelmed. He managed to close the door behind him without breaking our embrace. He lifted me into his arms and I surprised myself by wrapping my legs around his waist. I had decided to just let go of all inhibitions and enjoy this night. I needed this after all I had been through. He would be on break next week and then he only had two more weeks of school and I would never see him again, so I figured that this could be my one wild escapade in life. I pointed to my bedroom and he walked me into it and softly placed me on the bed. He took off his shirt and lay down next to me.

"Do you have condoms?" I cautiously asked him.

He chuckled at my obvious inexperience. "Yes darling, I do but we won't need them right now. I just want to lie here with you and hold you until you fall asleep. Do you mind that?"

Stunned, I didn't respond right away. I just knew that he was bursting from his seams to vacuum away my cemented cob webs. Was he playing mind games with me? My silence must have been obvious because he turned me to face him.

"Evelyn, don't judge me on my age alone. I am not here to fuck your brains out and then leave. You are a beautiful woman who has yet to experience true happiness for herself. It has always been on account of someone else being happy. I don't know what's going to happen with us in the future, but then again, who does? All I know is that I've had the opportunity to spend the evening with a smart, funny, talented, gorgeous woman who has humbled herself so much that she isn't aware of these things even as someone points them out to her. And she is giving me yet another chance to be in her personal space and I'm not about to ruin it over a quick lay. I know there's a lot for us to discover about one another but just allow me to be the gentleman that I am and take care of you for the night. Will you do that?"

I didn't respond. I just turned back over and wrapped his arm around my waist and fell asleep as he planted gentle kisses on my shoulder.

I was having the best sleep of my life when I felt a weird sensation; almost like I was peeing on myself. Coming to full consciousness, I jolted out of my slumber out of fear that at almost forty years old, I was still peeing in the bed. I looked down and realized quickly where the sensation was coming from. My legs were propped up onto Jacques' shoulders and he was hungrily making a feast out of my love nest. Without even looking up, he continued devouring me and in fact seemed to be getting more into it as my awareness set in and I began to verbally show my appreciation. For the next twenty minutes or so, he got up close and personal with my lady and they became the best of friends it seemed. And then, we made love for the rest of the morning and it was more than I could have ever imagined. I think I lost count at five orgasms and we were still going. Needless to say, this boy was definitely a man where it counted. He worked my body like it had never, and I do mean NEVER been worked before. Put me in positions that were almost humanly impossible. When we finally came up for air, I had broken out in a full out sweat and was gasping for air. We both lay side by side on our stomachs for about an hour not speaking; just basking in our post love making. He massaged my back and buttocks and planted kisses all over me. We showered together, which led to another love making session, then we ordered take out and watched movies. We laughed and chased each other around the house naked. I also helped him go over his lines for that night's show. I can honestly say that I had a great time with him. Before we knew it, it was almost five o' clock and he had to head back downtown to get ready for his show's second night. He invited me to go but I couldn't. I had a lot of work that needed to be completed before the next day; only the seniors and the fall students were on spring break, the winter students weren't so lucky.

"Well, I will call you when I'm done. I'd like to see you afterwards," he said, standing in my doorway kissing me on the neck.

"We'll see. It is a school night still for me, you know?" I said, starting to feel the uncertainty creep back up at the mention of school.

"You sound like a teacher," he teased.

"That's cause I am one," I teased back.

He looked me directly in the eyes and said, "I really enjoyed this day with you and look forward to spending many more with you. I was thinking that since your daughters are gone all week and I have the week off as well, maybe we could spend the week together. We don't have to go anywhere if you don't like. We could just spend the time here. I know your schedule is limited this week at school and I don't have any shows until the weekend; that definitely sounds great to me if you're ok with it."

"I thought you were going back home to visit your parents this week?"

"Yes, but they will be here in two weeks anyway. I could just not go," he said as he looked down at his watch. "Look, I've got to go. Think about it and I'll call you when the curtains go down tonight. See you later darling." He kissed me and ran down the steps.

I closed the door slowly and slid to the floor. "What have you gotten yourself into?" I said to myself as chills ran down my back.

"Hello my darling, this is Jacques. Just letting you know that the show went well. Had a great turn out from school. They all want to go out for drinks but I'd rather hold you in my arms. Give me a call when you get this message and I'll be right over."

"Evelyn? Is everything alright? This is Jacques calling. I called you last night as I said I would and you never returned my call. I just figured that you got caught up in work and fell asleep. Maybe you'll have time today. I'd really like to see you. Call me... please."

"Evelyn. Darling? Did I do something wrong? I've tried to not call so much but I'm worried. I know we never established whether we would be spending the week together but its Thursday already and I still want to see you. I'd like to know something. Ok?"

"Ok. I think I get it. I won't call anymore. But tell me this, do you really want happiness or are you content with bringing misery to yourself and those around you? You think we don't see the pain in your eyes when you come to school? All I wanted to do was mend it. But I guess you'd rather use the excuse that I'm too young and inexperienced than really take a chance. Your ex-husband was older and look at where that got you."

WHAT HAVE I GOTTEN MYSELF INTO?!

"Ms. Brown, Mr. Wellington is here to see you," my secretary said over the intercom.

I took a deep breath and said, "Send him in." It had been two weeks since I'd last seen or heard from Jacques. I know it was wrong the way I left him hanging but I just couldn't continue seeing him. I was starting to like the attention and care he displayed towards me and the lovemaking was like nothing I had experienced before with Gary. It was incredible. He made me laugh and our conversations were surprisingly filled with more than just the latest pop craze like most young people his age. But that brief love affair was just that; brief and an affair. Not only could I lose my job but I would embarrass myself if anyone ever found out that I was seeing a man almost twenty years younger than myself. A man who had no job and was still a student at the school I led. I mean, what could he possibly bring to my life? I already have two children to care for.

So tell me why my heart skipped a beat when he entered my office?

"Have a seat, Mr. Wellington," I said to him; trying my hardest to sound as professional and unemotional as possible.

"No, I'd rather stand. I'm not staying long, I have to head over for graduation rehearsal and I just wanted to speak my peace. I want you to know that in spite of your misjudgment of me, I do care for you. I may not be able to bring you all of the material and financial things that you need in your life, but I more than make up for them where it counts. And I'm not just talking about sex. I never saw you as a conquest. I had… Have a genuine interest in you Evelyn and would give anything to have the opportunity to express that. I have watched you from the first day in orientation and I have admired you and dreamed of being lucky enough to be close to you. When I had that chance, I told myself that I would not mess it up for anything. I would prove to you that you could find love again. Even in an unlikely source such as myself. I am not like most young men, Evelyn. You cannot deny that. You cannot deny that the time we spent together was great. We had great conversation. I'm not asking for your hand in marriage nor am I asking for commitment. All I'm asking is that you step out on a limb and give me a chance to prove to you. Whether right or wrong, give me that chance. You deserve to be treated like the queen that you have displayed yourself to be. Allow me the chance to do it; or not. My parents are here and I'll be spending the entire weekend with them in the city. They want me to go back to London with them on Monday. If I go, it'll be for good but I will stay, if you want me to. All you have to do is say so. I don't know what the future holds but I know I want you in it. After tomorrow, I am no longer under your instruction and therefore free to publicly see you. If you tell me that's what you want. So, are you willing to give me that opportunity?"

I was speechless. There were so many questions and rebuttals running through my head that it was giving me a headache. Part of me wanted to lock the door and strip him down naked but the other more sensible part of me wanted to dismiss him and let him get on that plane. "I don't know what to say," is all I could think of.

"Say what you feel, my darling," he said.

"I'm sorry, Jacques. I just can't."

"Got it. Well thank you for your time, Ms. Brown. See you at tomorrow's graduation." Like a puppy that just lost his owner, he hung his head and shook it as if to say he understood. He turned and reached for the door.

"Wait!" I yelled out at him.

Evelyn Brown, what the hell have you gotten yourself into?

SEX

The Sex Club

Sharon

So few people are blessed enough to find a true friend in life, so when I was fortunate enough to find two of them, I knew that I had something special. Although three completely different personalities and from three different walks of life, my best friends and I have formed a bond that most only dream of. We have all been through our own share of ups and downs and have supported one another through them all. Being the only child, these women have served as sisters to me and in fact have been unofficially inducted into the Jones family tree; according to my mother.

Lisa has been my best friend the longest. We met in junior high school and ironically hated each other at first. We met in the seventh grade and pretty much wished death on each other. Twenty years later, neither she nor I could tell you why we hated each other so much but my guess is because we were so much alike that maybe we saw each other as competition. When she and I joined the little league cheerleading squad the following year I think we realized that there was power in numbers and therefore decided to join forces, and the rest has been a beautiful friendship. She and her husband Carl have been married for three years now and she has already caught the "Housewives of Baltimore" syndrome. She has decided that since her husband is the president of the Moorestone Banking firm's marketing department in Annapolis and he provides them with a very lush lifestyle that she can just stop her career altogether. She and I argued for months about that, especially since she has a master's degree in education and she was making a stable living as a professor at Towson University. For the life of me, I just couldn't understand how or why a very intelligent woman would give up her life for a man, even if he were her husband. I just don't think it wise to totally depend on anyone for your basic survival needs. But after twenty years of friendship, I know when to just stay quiet and let her do her own thing because as head strong and steadfast as we both are, some battles between us are just meant to not be fought.

We met Qiana in college at Bowie State University our junior year. Although only a freshman, she had managed to make her presence known and quickly built a reputation for herself. Qiana is what we would call, "Ghetto fabulous"; gorgeous girl with long legs and a face that looked like it could easily be on the cover of Vogue but her attitude was total hood. She was loud, obnoxious, and very opinionated. We met her in the most unorthodox way imaginable; we caught her in bed with Lisa's boyfriend at the time. I remember that day vividly. When Lisa confronted her, Qiana maintained a smug and almost proud look on her face which set Lisa off. Now I've never been a believer in women whose men cheat on them and they insist on going after the other woman but the way she acted as if she didn't care that my friend was hurting, I totally understood and joined in. For months we talked about her to everyone who would listen and branded her the campus slut. But the thing that jarred us was that she did not care. It was as if she embraced her new found fame and we were just fueling it. We noticed that with each bad thing that was said about her, more guys seemed to flock to her and even some girls started befriending her just so that they could get the same attention she had. After awhile, people started looking at us as if we were jealous of her, which was far beyond the truth so Lisa and I decided that we would have a heart to heart with the infamous woman. We confronted her after her dance practice one day.

"If it isn't Thelma and Louise, here to wreak havoc on every young freshman girl's life," she laughed as she walked up to us.

"Look, we wanted to come to you as women and talk about things. Its starting to get out of hand," I said, a bit agitated at her continued attitude.

"Talk about what? I don't owe you anything? And neither do you," she said folding her arms in front of her chest.

Out of the two of us, Lisa was the more level headed one as I was known to blow my fuse very easily so when she said that, Lisa stepped in and took over the conversation before I did something that would ruin my chance of graduating with honors. "We just wanted to say that we apologize for spreading those rumors about you. We don't know you and have no right to come at you like that. It was just that, I really liked Keith and it hurt my heart that he would do that to me and as a fellow sista, it hurt me that you acted like you didn't care," Lisa sincerely said.

"You know what troubles me about us, SISTAS? It's the lack of respect we have for ourselves and one another. We let these men treat us any kind of way they want, all the while we are catering to him hand and foot. We blame and fight one another for stealing each other's men but what we fail to realize is if he was truly all about you, he would not have ALLOWED himself to be stolen. No one can steal an unwilling person; that's called rape, and I'm not so sure there are a lot of men walking around here getting their dicks sucked forcefully. You said you got mad at me because I acted like I didn't care but you knew your boyfriend was no good way before you caught me on my knees in front of him and yet you did nothing. So if you would allow yourself to not care about what's in front of you, why should I? I can't do for you what you are not willing to do for yourself. You all called me a slut and said that I lacked respect for myself. When truthfully, I totally love and respect myself and never fake to anyone about who I am. I love men, and I love having sex. You have only seen me with one man and have automatically branded me. What does that say to your fellow SISTA? That if you love your body enough to share it with a man whom you have a mutual attraction towards, that youre a slut?" She shook her head before concluding, "Have a good day ladies. And before you go off trying to throw someone in the mud, find out what they're about first," she turned and walked away. Before she got to far away, she turned and added, "And for the record, he has been pursuing me all year and I wouldn't give in cause I knew yall were together but he told me yall broke up. So when you came bursting through the door with that sad look on your face, I actually felt proud because I helped to force open your eyes to the reality that you refused to face. And just so you know, my name's Qiana."

And that was how we strangely became friends with the feisty yet confident Qiana. We would see her around campus and as the months progressed, took to her for her ability to stand up for herself and not apologize for it. Although very different from Lisa and me, Qiana has brought a wonderful dynamic to our group. She's probably the most sincere person I've ever met and can hurt your feelings and tell you she loves you all in one breath. She dropped out of college her sophomore year and hopped from job to job until finally deciding on a career as a make up artist. She currently owns her own beauty and spa salon that is actually doing really well. She's never been married and jokingly blames marriage for all the violence in the Middle East. For as long as I've known her, she hasn't even had a boyfriend. She has what she calls BAMs, which stands for Build-A-Man; she believes that if you make a list of the qualities you want in the perfect man and then go out and find one man to fit each quality, you can Build-A-Man. And to my surprise, in my eleven years of knowing this woman, she has actually had much success. She has the sensitive guy, whom she can talk to when she needs a good shoulder to cry on; the money guy who actually helped her to get through beauty school and open her shop last year; the adventurous guy, who takes her on these crazy trips that you only see on the discovery channel; the guy with the trade, who this time around is an executive private chef; and the sex guy. You gotta have the sex guy. Some may say that she is living a reckless lifestyle but it has managed to work for her and she actually lives a very drama free life. She is totally honest with these men about her desire to remain just where they are in their relationship and it seems as though these men who just want to be around her, oblige. The very few who do not cooperate are quickly dismissed and replaced as if they never were. No matter what your opinions are towards Qiana and her chosen lifestyle, there is no doubt that she handles her business and has seemed to have found the secret to a stress free life. In spite of our abstract initial encounter, Lisa and I have come to really love and depend on Qiana's colorful personality.

And what about me and my love life, you might ask? Well, we'll get to me later but for right now I was preparing to host our weekly Sex Club meeting. And no I'm not talking about one of those toy buying parties, it's more like a Book Club but instead of discussing books, we discuss, give advice, and address any issues or concerns that one or all of us are having with our partners in the bedroom. It's kind of like being in a room with Dr. Phil, Dr. Ruth, and a porn star; it gets pretty intense sometimes. We have only been meeting for a month but so far the meetings have ended with all of us rushing home to put it on our men, so I decided to REALLY make this week interesting by trying something new.

My friends all arrived around the same time and by the looks on their faces, I could tell that they couldn't wait to get the meeting started.

"Hello ladies. This week's Sex Club will now begin," I proudly said.

"Ok, Honorable Judge Mathis," Qiana teased.

"HA. HA. HA. Anyway, as I told you two during the week, I would be doing something different this meeting."

"Are we going to practice the art of dick sucking? Cause if so, move aside honey and let ME host this meeting today" Qiana proudly said, jumping up from her spot on the couch.

Lisa chimed in, "Please Qiana, must you always refer to it as a…"

"As a what Lisa? A what? Say it. Say dick. D-I-C-K, dick. Not penis but dick," Qiana teased Lisa's reluctance to ever talk dirty or sexual. Lisa threw one of my throw pillows at Qiana and tried to hide her embarrassment.

"I'm so excited about today's meeting because I want us to take our sex lives to the next level." I excitedly said. "Ladies, we are all successful in our lives; great careers, families, friendships but we are all struggling in our love lives and that's not right. I want each of us to feel sexually free enough to express ourselves openly to our men. No more just lying there and taking it but being able to give it as well."

"Speak for yourself honey, cause my sex life is FIYA!!" Qiana said snapping her fingers at me.

"Well that maybe true but there's more to sex than just the physical contact of it," I said to her.

"In what world?! Sex is ALL physical honey," she said as she started to gyrate her hips.

"And that, my dear is all the more reason why I came up with this week's topic," I said

"Alright already, spill the beans! I've waited all week to hear this big plan," Lisa squealed.

"Ok, ok, well after last meeting's discussion, I came to the conclusion that we have to do more than just talk about our problems and concerns in bed. We have to actually take some action. Instead of discussing how unsatisfied we are or how bored we are, let's do something about it!"

"And what exactly did you have in mind?" Lisa asked a little less excited as I'm sure she wasn't prepared to really make too many drastic changes in her bedroom.

"Well, we've all agreed to keep our Sex Club a secret from our partners, right?" They both nodded in agreement. "Well, I'd like to take this secret one step further. I'd like for each of us to role play this week." I stopped to survey my friends' faces; Lisa looked as if she were about to have a heart attack and Qiana was grinning ear to ear.

"YES! I love playing the school teacher who has the naughty student who needs to be taught a lesson," Qiana beamed.

"Hold fast, Quick Draw McGraw. This isn't going to be your typical role playing. This will be an activity to help us step outside of our comfort zones and experience other avenues of pleasure. So first off, the characters that you will be performing for your man will be given to you by someone else in the group. The character has to be someone completely opposite of the real you. Someone that in a million years, you would never be. Second, you must be this character for the entire week until next Tuesday night. Third, you are not to tell your partner that you are role playing, you must maintain secrecy about the club as we promised. If he starts asking questions as to why the sudden change, just give him the kind of response you think your character would give. And last, next Tuesday night you are to ask your partner for feedback on some of the changes he's seen in you the past week. Ask him what he liked, what he didn't like, and how you compared this week to how you normally are. And when we get together next week we will discuss our results and what we learned about ourselves and our partners from this activity." Again I stopped and surveyed my friends' faces and they both looked like they wanted to slap the living daylights out of me.

"So wait, let me get this straight, you want one of you two to come up with a character for me to be and walk around for a WEEK acting like I'm some made up character JUST to make my partner happy?! Fuck that! I don't like that nigga THAT much!" Qiana said, clearly annoyed with my revelation.

"Come on Qee, be a team player. You agreed also that you could use a little more adventure in your already adventurous sex life. This could be fun if you really let go and let your character lead you," I practically begged, wanting my friends to really believe in my vision for this activity.

After a few moments, Qiana said, "Ok fine. And you said one of us gets to pick the other's role?"

"Correct," I said.

"Well I want to pick Lisa's," she beamed, grinning mischievously at Lisa.

"Oh no, no, no. I do NOT want YOU picking ANYTHING sexual for me! Absolutely not!" Lisa refused.

"Be a team player Lisa," Qiana mocked.

"Sharon?" Lisa pleaded to me.

"Lisa, please honey," I pleaded back.

Taking a deep breath, "Fine," she huffed, "What is it?"

Still smiling ear to ear, Qiana said, "You will be the dominatrix!"

"WHAT?!! Oh my goodness, I don't know anything about that! How in the H E double hockey sticks am I supposed to be a dominatrix for a whole week? I knew you were going to pick something crazy!"

"Did she just spell out HELL?" Qiana asked with a crooked face.

"Qiana, hush. It's actually not crazy, Lisa. That's actually perfect for you! You don't necessarily have to go around dressed in a leather bodysuit all week but embody the mentality of a dominatrix; the control, the passion, and the dominance. You've voiced to us how you feel Carl doesn't listen to you, how you feel like a mouse and he's a lion. Well now is your chance to be that lioness and whip his ass into shape! This is more of a mentality role playing. So once you embody the mentality of the sexual dominatrix, you will be able to easily transition that into your sex life."

"Goodness. I don't know, Sharon," she said, nervously rubbing her hands back and forth up her thighs.

"Lisa, you and I both know that you have always had issues with speaking up for yourself to men. You're very confident and head strong but when it comes to speaking up for yourself to them, you become a ball of clay," I said lovingly to my friend.

"Ain't that the truth! Don't forget how we met," Qiana blurted out.

"Ok miss mouth almighty, I'm going to pick yours myself. You're going to play the role of the virgin," I smirked. Lisa burst out into laughter at that one.

"HA! Fat chance! I'm sorry, but I'm way past that honey."

"Exactly. I think you have gotten so far past it that you wrap sex around every encounter you have with a man."

"I do no-, well, ok but so what? I thought this was an activity about creating a better and more adventurous sex life. How is NOT having sex going to accomplish that?" she argued.

"We all know that you can get it on the regular but I think you are missing one key ingredient to having a great sex life; substance. I think you've gotten so far past the virginal state of mind that you have never been able to experience a relationship without sex. So for a week, I'd like for you to embody the mentality of the virgin. Take one of your BAMs and spend the week with only him. Allow him to take you out, talk to him on the phone, anything but no physical contact."

"WHAT?! No sex for a week?! I don't even wait seven days during that time of the month! Aunt Flow comes to town for three days, I take the fourth to recuperate and by the fifth I'm backing it up on someone's grown son," she proudly admitted.

"Good! Look Qee, you're not getting any younger and I'm not trying to criticize or change you. I love you totally for who you are but this is meant to help each of us to experience and overall intense, gratifying, and LASTING sex life," I reassured her.

"Geez, so you mean to tell me that the only way for me to have a better sex life than the already fabulous one I have is to just not have sex at all? Either I have the greatest sex life ever or I need to see a shrink."

"Aww honey, its not that. I think this is wonderful for you," Lisa said, trying to caress Qiana's ego. "Saving yourself for the right man is what God wants from us women. Sharon's not trying to insult you. This is all to open our eyes to see our lives in a better light."

"Never thought I'd see the day when Lisa would be given permission to have more sex then me," Qiana said, shaking her head in disbelief. "Wait, what about you? It's your turn now. Looks like little Miss Cat Woman over there is going to get her chance to take a jab back at you Sharon. Gotta see this, where's my popcorn?"

"Ok, have at it," I confidently said.

Lisa stared at me and titled her head from side to side as if she were really studying me. She even dramatically put her hand on her chin and rubbed it as she contemplated her choice. After what seemed like an unnecessarily long time, she finally shouted, "Got it! For this week, you are to be the Slave!"

"The slave?"

"Oh shit! That's a good one girl!" Qiana said high fiving Lisa. "Yes, because you are used to being the leader; always being in control of every situation, including your men. And I know that you say you find it hard to meet a man who is as successful in his career as he is in bed but I personally believe it's because you find it hard to allow a man to be just that, a man."

"And so with your guy Craig, you must allow him for a week to take control. Especially in the bedroom. You are not to pay for anything, tell him where you want to go, or make any decisions. You have to be at his beckon call all week. And in the bed you have to lay there and take it," Lisa said, covering her mouth as she tried to suppress her girlish giggle.

"Put yourself in a submissive and vulnerable position this week. Give him a lot of 'Yes daddy' and 'Whatever you say big poppa'," Qiana grinned.

"But he's already used to my dominating ways. And he's cool with that," I protested.

"Is he?" Qiana snidely asked. "Trust me; if you fall back, he will step up. If he doesn't then you need to drop that loser."

I took a deep breath as I realized that I had brought this on myself and that I was sure they had felt the very same way I was feeling just a few moments ago so I had no choice but to oblige; it was my idea after all. "Ok fine, as long as you all promise to keep your character's integrity, I do too."

"Promise!" They both said in unison.

This was looking to be a very interesting week and it hadn't even begun. I just had to go and open my big mouth. I wished that I could control time and go back thirty minutes and cancel this meeting.

Lisa AKA Dominatrix

Sharon had to be out of her cotton picking mind if she thought being some dominating woman would fly with my already dominating husband. When I met Carl five years ago, it was definitely a love at first sight situation. Being ten years my senior, he had already been well established in his banking career and was finally looking to settle down and get married. We met in the grocery store, of all places, and his deep Barry White like voice immediately heightened my senses. Although only thirty six at the time, he was starting to grey at the roots of his hair and goatee and for some reason that made him even more attractive. He spoke very confidently as if there were no doubt in his mind that I would one day soon belong to him. Playing hard to get with this no nonsense man was out of the question. He took me out and wined and dined me. Not being very sexually experienced, he brought me to my first orgasm and showed me around the bedroom in a way that left me breathless every time. He made it very clear early on what his intentions were and that he was not looking for a fling; he was looking for marriage. After only two months of dating, he and I started seeing each other exclusively and after a year and a half, he proposed. He would have proposed sooner had I not practically begged him to wait. Truth be told, he pretty much called all of the shots in our relationship; which I didn't mind one bit. I prided myself on being able to find a man who knew what his role was in the relationship. That's why when he presented to me his desire for me to no longer work after we got married, I quickly obeyed. Our vows do say "honor and obey", don't they? Carl is the head of our household and whatever he needs and wants, I am there to fulfill it. Please do not misunderstand, my husband is very loving towards me and treats me like a Queen but there can only be one lion in the den. So for Sharon to propose that I sort of take over was totally absurd to me but I had made a promise to the girls and if I had expected them to uphold their ends of the bargain, well so should I. I just had absolutely no idea how.

The first five days were a disaster. I had no idea what I was doing. I kept trying to pick fights with him or boss him around but he just kept blowing me off. He questioned if my period was early and offered to get me some Midol. I was turning into a fumbling fool. Day five was the highlight of this disastrous week. My husband doesn't get much free time as his job demands a lot from him so he looks forward to his Sunday night football games. He completely shuts the world out and locks himself away in his man cave and won't resurface until the very last game is over. He makes it very clear that unless the house is burning down and is about to collapse on top of him, DO NOT DISTURB. So when I heard him yell out in disgust at the referee on the screen for making a bad call, I almost had a change of heart. Hind sight is 20/20, they say.

"Honey," I whispered as I tapped on the door lightly. When no response came, I took a deep breath and cracked the door open. His back was towards the door and he didn't budge from his position on the edge of the couch. He nearly sent me flying backwards as he jumped up and started screaming for the guy running with the ball on the screen to "GO! GO! GO!" Carl is an extremely mild mannered and even keeled man who doesn't show much emotion, except when it comes to football. I secretly wished that I could excite him like that. As the guy on the screen ran to the end of the field, Carl started screaming in excitement and even went up to the television screen and kissed it. When he turned back to sit down, we locked eyes and his smiled disappeared.

"Why are you just standing in the doorway?" he asked with a puzzled look on his face.

It was now or never, I thought, so I stepped into the room and closed the door. "I want to watch football," I said as I approached the couch and grabbed a beer from the mini refrigerator he had in the room.

"Since when do you like football or beer?" he questioned, still standing up.

"Well since you never bothered to ask; I've liked football for awhile now and a girl can enjoy a little brew every once in a while, can't she?"

"Yea ok. You're up to something, what do you want?" He sat down and took the beer out of my hand and opened it for me. Before I could answer, he turned back to the TV and I knew he had tuned me out. If I were to declare my dominance, now would be the perfect time. Or so I thought. I jumped up and stood right in front of the television and I thought I saw my husband's head spin. He yelled at me, "WHAT ARE YOU DOING?! MOVE OUT OF THE WAY!" When I didn't adhere to his subtle request, he jumped up and grabbed me by the waist and said, "Have you lost your mind Lisa?!" I tried to wrap my arms around his neck and kiss him but he avoided my kiss. "What is wrong with you woman? What has gotten into you lately?!" I reached for his sweat pants and tried to pull them down but he stepped back away from my grasp. "What the hell is wrong with you?" I knew he was pissed because he only cursed when he was mad but I couldn't back down, I had to keep going to prove myself. He sat down shaking his head and tried to resume watching the game. "You are really off your rocker right now Lisa and I suggest you go back and find it," he said as if he were letting me know that this ordeal was over. I pretended to walk towards the door but walked behind the couch instead. In one swift motion, I reached down from behind him and grabbed a hold of his penis through his sweat pants and he jumped up in surprise and head butt me in the nose. I fell to the floor as the agonizing pain shot through my nose and down my spine.

"OWWWWWWW! My nose!" I screamed out in pain.

"Shit! Lisa, you scared the hell out of me!" he said as he came around to the back of the couch and knelt in front of me. He lifted my chin with his hand and said, "I don't think it's broken but I'll go get you some ice. What has gotten into you? Why would you do that when I'm watching the game?" He walked to the refrigerator and put some ice in a paper towel and brought it to me. "Here, put this on there and tilt your head back." He picked me up and sat me on the couch. "Now please, sit there in silence as I try to enjoy the remaining minutes of this game or are there any other senseless tricks you have up your sleeve that you want to ruin my only day off with?" he said with a look of half disgust and half concern before turning again to watch the game; this time, turning the volume way up.

Who was I kidding; this stupid activity would never work. I spent the remainder of the next day nursing my bruised nose. He and I hadn't said as much as two words to one another and I knew that with only one more day of this activity, there was no way I was going to accomplish this goal. It had been over a week since we last had sex and that was a quickie so at the rate we were going, it didn't look like he and I would be taking a roll in the hay for awhile. Feeling defeated, I decided to just give it a rest. It would have been nice to have been able to show a different side of me to my husband but it just wouldn't work out that way. He married me for the characteristics that I already displayed, not some mysterious trait that was just lying dormant, waiting to be released.

When Tuesday came, I had prepared to cook his favorite lasagna dish and finally reveal to him why I had been acting so strange these past seven days. Before I could pull out the pots and pans, he called and told me that he would be in the office working late. I offered to bring him a warm plate and he accepted, not being able to resist my cooking. I arrived at his building around eight thirty and noticed that other than his car, there were only about five other cars in the huge one hundred plus space parking lot. I checked in with security and ascended twenty-two floors in the elevator to his executive floor. Once I reached his floor, I saw that his secretary was not at her desk and from the looks of things, no one else was at theirs either. I walked through the glass doors and turned down the long hall towards his office. I passed the VP's office which was unoccupied as well and came to a stop in front of Carl's closed door. I took another look around me and suddenly became very aware that he and I were the only two on this whole entire floor and that the other cars I saw outside were probably the security guards and cleaning crew scattered throughout this twenty-five floor building. A weird feeling started creeping up my back as I reevaluated the situation. This was the last day for my Sex Club activity and up to this point; I realized that I had been approaching it totally wrong. Being dominant didn't mean being a bitch or forceful. My husband didn't get to this position by being a jerk to everyone; aside from his hard work and credentials, he got this big office on the twenty-second floor by being confident, sure of himself and his ability to lead others. He didn't win over my heart by forcing his dominance down my throat, he just was confident in what he had to offer and didn't worry so much about whether I would accept it or not. This whole week, I had become a blubbering fool all because I worried more about the result than I did my own actions. As I knocked on his office door, I felt a foreign sensation and a surge of energy that I had never felt around my husband. When he opened the door, I surveyed him for the first time in years. For a forty one year old man, he still oozed sex appeal and had a very

"Billy Dee Williams" aurora about him like he could have easily been a stand in for those Colt 45 commercials. We had a gym at home that he worked out in religiously and it showed. His tie was undone and the top few buttons of his shirt were unbuttoned to show off his few coils of hair. His slacks were tailored to fit his body just perfectly and my mouth began to water as I knew the secret that they held underneath. I guess I had been staring too long between his legs because he crossed his arms in front of himself.

"Hello? How are you? Nice to see you again," he playfully said in his low bass tone, kissing me on the forehead.

I glanced up at him with a smirk on my face and said, "Oh sorry. I forgot for a second why I was here."

"You sure you're feeling alright because you've been really weird all week," he said stepping aside so that I could come into the office.

"I'm feeling perfectly well honey," I said placing his food on the coffee table and then throwing my purse and coat onto the couch in front of it. He opened the foil that covered the food and inhaled deeply. He pulled one of the side chairs close to the coffee table and began to devour his meal without even glancing up.

"Mmmm, I haven't eaten all day and this definitely makes it all worth it," he said with a mouth full of food. I smiled as he enjoyed my labor. I glanced out his floor to ceiling windows that ran all along his back wall and was thankful that we were so far up because he had no blinds or curtains to hide what I was about to do. I unbuttoned my sweater and threw it at him. Startled, he looked up in disbelief as I stood there now undoing the buttons on my jeans.

"Lisa, what are you doing?" he asked. His voice questioned but his eyes, his eyes said it all. He was excited.

Stepping back into my heels, I walked over to him with nothing on but my bra and panties. Good thing I had purchased this new set earlier in the week and didn't let them go to waste. As I stood in front of him with my hands on my hips, he sat back in the chair with a look of amazement in his eyes. I took the loose tie from around his neck and walked behind him.

"What are you doing, love?" he said again, trying to turn to look at me but I pulled him back down into his seat.

"Shh. Relax baby. You just sit there and let me be the boss for a change," I confidently said, surprising myself.

"This is crazy," he said but didn't move a muscle as I massaged his shoulders. Once he began to relax, I grabbed each of his arms and held them behind his back.

I tied his hands together with his tie and secured them to the back of the chair with the remaining fabric. I came back around to face him and he had the unmistakable look of lust on his face. I straddled him and stared him square in the face. "Who are you and what have you done with my wife?" he smirked.

"Be quiet. Tonight, I make all the calls. I call all the shots and you just sit there and take it like a good boy. Got it?" Who the hell was I and where did this person come from all of the sudden? I guess the slight change in altitude had affected my inhibitions.

Totally expecting him to be uncooperative, he surprised me and said, "Yes ma'am," and bit the bottom of his lip. I grabbed his bottom lip with my teeth and gently pulled on it until he released it from his teeth. I sucked on his lip for a few until he couldn't stand it anymore and kissed me back. Our kiss intensified and we started thrusting into each other through our clothes. When I heard myself moan, I knew that I had to stop before I lost control and failed the activity yet again. I broke our kiss and stood up. The look on Carl's face was priceless. I walked over to the couch and sat down with my legs spread open. I undid my bra and threw it at him. I began to massage my breasts as I knew my husband had always been a fan of my large D's. When I brought one nipple to my mouth and began licking it, he let out an exaggerated breath as if he were holding it the whole time. Releasing my right breast, I traced a finger down my stomach and into my panties where I found my small mound of heaven. As I began to gently rub back and forth across it, my fingers became soaked in my flowing juices. Never being an avid masturbator, I found it easy to get into and soon was shoving two fingers into my tight walls. I couldn't help but to scream out to my husband my enjoyment as I pleasured myself. Totally engulfed in what I was doing, he was speechless as he tilted his head to the side, still biting on his bottom lip. As I reached my peak, I announced to the entire building that I had arrived at my ultimate point of pleasure. When I had calmed down enough, I stood up again and took my panties off. I walked back over to where he was seated and I knelt down in between his legs and began to unfasten his slacks.

"I don't know what I did to deserve this attention but please help me to keep getting it," he said, looking down at me.

"Be quiet I said! You are not to speak unless spoken to. Understand?"

"Yes... Ma'am," he barely uttered as I took him in my mouth and began to work my magic. I enjoyed pleasing my husband and had become very good at giving him oral pleasure, so tonight I wanted to be sure that I put in extra effort to make him feel great. I moved up and down his shaft ensuring that I made it as slippery as possible. I smiled to myself as I saw his eyes roll back into his head and his mouth hang open. I got into a rhythm as he started to thrust his hips towards me, sending trickles of his fruit down my throat. Grunting and struggling to get his hands free from the Girls Scout knot I tied his hands in, he said, "Free my hands baby. Please. I want to fuck you up against the wall. Please." Hearing my mild mannered husband speak to me in that way made me whimper. I wanted so badly to do what he said, but this was my time to show my control so I refused to give in.

Releasing him from my mouth, I stood up and said, "I see someone doesn't know how to listen." I pulled his pants all the way down to his ankles and straddled him doggie style. I teased him by placing the head of his penis at the opening of my lady. When he tried to thrust into me, I moved away.

"Ok love. Ok. Whatever you say. Just please don't tease me," he whined.

"You want me to put it in?" I said, playing with myself.

"Yes love."

"Are you going to listen to what mama says?"

"Yes mama."

"Good boy," I said, leaning in to kiss him passionately before turning again and placing his throbbing thick member into me. As I slowly lowered down onto him, a mixture of pain and pleasure surged through my body as my husband's large size filled my little frame completely. I started a slow circular motion and he began to push himself into me at the same pace. I leaned back into him and we continued our slow dance together. "Yes Carl. Oh my God, you feel so good." This role playing was bringing on a new found confidence that I never knew I could have around him and was causing me to say and do some unbelievable things. But from the sound of my husband's moans in my ear behind me, I doubt he would complain.

He too had never been much of a very boisterous lover but I guess from the excitement of the whole situation, he was also feeling free to express himself. "Oooh Lisa, baby you feel good too." I gasped when he said that and it made me thrust faster back into him and he matched my speed yet again. I turned to face him, never losing my connection with him. I grabbed his neck and began bouncing on top of him. I reached behind him and untied the knot that bound his hands together. I wanted to feel his strong hands gripping at my waist and shoving me down into his engorged penis; which is exactly what he did once his hands became free. We made love all over his office and he even held me up to the wall and pounded away into me as we knocked his pictures off the wall. We ended an hour and a half later on the couch in a heap of sweat. He held me in his arms and combed through my hair with his fingers.

"So are you going to tell me what's going on with you?" he finally said to me.

"You didn't enjoy it?" I said to him, feeling my insecurities creep back.

"HELL YEA I enjoyed it!" he laughed. "But in the five years of knowing you, three of which you have bore my name, I have NEVER seen you act the way you did tonight." So I explained to him about our Sex Club and this week's activity and why I had been acting weird all week. "Well that explains it but why do you feel like you need an activity to be open like that with me?" he questioned.

"I don't know. You've just always been the dominant one and I've respected you for that."

"Yes but I've always wanted you to feel like you have a say in what goes on between us, Lisa. I am a man who is sure of what he wants in life and you are my wife who I thought felt the same. Do you think I married you because I thought I could dominate you?"

"I'm not saying that. I'm just saying that you are used to being in a leadership position and therefore there is really no room for another one."

"Lisa no, that's not it at all. I don't see myself as a leader or ruler or even superior over you. You are my equal. When I asked you to stop working, it wasn't because I felt threatened that you would become successful, it was simply because I knew what no one did. You were unhappy. You didn't really care for your job and all you did was complain, so I figured, why not put you out of your misery and allow you to be free. But that was based off of what you showed me, not what I forced on you. And I didn't force you, I asked you. Any decision we've ever made, we made as a team, love. I have noticed over the years that you have become a bit meek and I just thought it was a growing phase you were going through and you would soon be out of it and back to the woman I fell in love with. That's why I've been giving you your space."

"Really? I was always so soft spoken around men but I initially thought that because you were older that you wanted a more mature woman, so I tried to loosen up and speak up more. But the more I got to know you and your character, the more I thought that I was wrong and that you wanted the softer me. I thought that you hated when I voiced my opinion or challenged your thoughts. "

"Are you crazy?! Woman the first time I fell in love with you was when we had that debate about whether or not the government was really God and when you got in my face I just wanted to strip you naked and take you right then and there. You were a challenge to me. I didn't care about the age difference. I wasn't going out seeking some young naïve girl because that wasn't you by a long shot but for some reason you became that once we got married. But I've been patient with you."

"So you mean to tell me that our whole marriage as been a bore because of me?" I said in total surprise at what he was saying to me.

"I wouldn't say all of that but I do think that we both were walking on two different paths," he smiled at me.

"So going forward, what would you like to see from me that you saw tonight? And what wouldn't you?"

"Well first of all, what you displayed the first six days of this week; never, I repeat, NEVER bring that clumsy clown around me ever!" he laughed as he playfully tickled me. "And second, what I saw tonight was what I saw the first time we met, the first time we went out, and the first time we made love. I saw confidence and not only a willingness to please me but a desire to enjoy that pleasure yourself. It was like you didn't care how I would react, you just went for it. And that turned me on. Seeing you please yourself made me lose my breath. I would love to experience that feeling every night with you if you gave me the chance. I wish you would display that towards me everyday. I love being around you my love but not while you're in this little mouse game you've been in. I'd rather you be the cat and come chase me around the house."

"Oh yea? You want the cat, huh?" I playfully said as I got up and stood directly above his face. "Well here baby, here comes the cat," I said as I lowered myself onto my husband's face.

Qiana AKA the Virgin

If my friends think that I'm going to go a whole week without having sex, then they must not really know me at all. Sex is like therapy to me. It calms my nerves, eases my pains, keeps me from having to go to the gym, and not to mention the wonders it does for my skin. So I know that I told the girls that I would go along with this little game of theirs but like the wise woman my mother is has said; what a person doesn't know won't hurt them.

As soon as I left the meeting, I hit the speed dial on my phone and called one of my BAMs, Maurice. Honey has a body to die for and being Haitian, his chiseled features and dark complexion made him irresistible to women. Most women, that is. Don't get me wrong, brother is fly but I've never been the one to sweat any man. And besides, if I ever did decide to mess up my life and settle down, he definitely would not be top on the list. See, while he's got it all right in the looks department, honey baby is a scrub. I've known him for about four months now and brother man has had at least eight jobs. He says its cause the economy isn't kind to the black man so all he can get are these temp construction jobs. Every time he goes on his "the black man is oppressed" rant; I just strip down naked so that he can quickly shut the hell up. I'd rather hear him talk about how wet I am than how Martin Luther King's dream isn't blah blah blah. The caliber of men I'm used to associating myself with typically all have a net worth of at least a half of a million; and that's the low ballers. So why do I continue to put myself through the ringer with this man you ask? Because where Maurice lacks in bank roll, he more than generously makes up for in the bedroom. When I say he has me climbing the walls like I'm trying out for Spiderman, I ain't never lied. It's like he skipped all his aptitude classes in school and went straight for Sex Ed. I have never screamed so loud or came so many times in one sex session without faking in my life. And of course, the man is packing. So if these heifers think that I'm going to stay away from all of that, they got another thing coming.

"What's up, gal?" he said on the other end of the receiver in his strong Haitian accent.

"Nothing much. What are you doing? I'm trying to come over," I said, getting straight to the point.

"You sure don't play around, do you?" he laughed.

"When have I ever?"

"True that. Come on over then. My roommate is out of town anyway."

Oh yeah, and that my friends, is another reason why he and I could never be more than friends with sexual benefits.

When I pulled up to his apartment complex, I glanced around his neighborhood for the first time. Normally, I try to be discreet and get in and get out without being spotted by anyone I may know but something suddenly came over me and I got curious. Being from the city, I rarely ventured onto this side of town. On my side of town, there would still be little nappy head kids running around outside although it was almost midnight. The dope boys would be making their nightly rounds and the hoochie mamas would be heading out to the clubs to find their next money maker; kind of like how I started out. But this area of Baltimore was almost like a whole different country. The streets were lined with trees, the grass was green and well kept, and it was quiet. The only noise you heard was from the occasional car that drove by. Maurice didn't really come off as the quiet county resident. From his demeanor and status, I definitely took him for a "my side of the town" kind of guy. Come to think of it, in the four months of knowing him, I never really had an in depth conversation with him. I met him at a VIP event at the Marriott and we got a room the same night. He's tried to tell me a little about his life but I never paid much attention. I started to wonder what would happen if I did entertain Sharon's crazy Sex Club activity and actually tried to get to know this man, without sex. I couldn't believe I was actually considering it. Maybe I was just sex deprived. I heard lack of it can do something to your mental stability, so I quickly locked my car and sped walked to his apartment.

"Took you long enough," he said, already standing in the doorway with nothing on but a pair of jeans. Damn, this man was fine as all hell. I responded by pushing him into his apartment, pinning him to the wall and undoing his pants that immediately fell to the floor displaying all of the glory that I'd come to know. Just as I was about to kneel in front of it and work my magic, that nagging feeling came over me. You know the feeling where you know you're about to do something that you shouldn't; something that you promised you wouldn't. Damn it! Why did I have to have such sexually deprived friends who like to rain on my sex parade?! I slumped to the ground like a spoiled kid that had just gotten their favorite toy taken from them.

"What's a matter, bay?" he asked half pissed and half surprised as I had never halted our sexcapades before for any reason.

Taking a deep breath and staring almost face to penis, I asked, "What's your last name?"

At first he just stared blank face at me, and then said, "You stopped to ask me what my last name is?"

All I could do was shrug. I felt as stupid as I'm sure I looked and sounded.

"Francois. Maurice Francois. What's yours?" he asked with genuine interest as he sat down next to me on the floor.

"Fontain. Qiana Fontain."

"Nice to meet you Qiana," he laughed. I had to laugh too; I guess it was a bit of an awkward and absurd situation to be in. Sexing someone for months and not even knowing their last name.

"Want to go to dinner with me tomorrow," I blurted out.

What the hell. What's one week?

We agreed to meet at Ruth's Chris Steakhouse downtown the next day. Not quite my cup of tea but he was paying so I definitely wouldn't turn it down. True to form, I was forty five minutes late; my mother always said, if a man isn't willing to wait, he wasn't worth the rushing anyway. As the hostess escorted me to our table, I was expecting him to chew me out about my tardiness but instead, he just stood up, kissed me on the cheek and whispered in my ear, "You look beautiful." For the first time, I was speechless around him and it wasn't because I had a mouth full of him either. He cleaned up well. His chiseled body was neatly camouflaged underneath a striped button up shirt which was tucked into grey slacks. Although not tailored made, his outfit fit him like a glove but not too tight. His shoes definitely were Stacy Adams, probably from Macy's, but with his income I let them pass. He actually looked just as sexy with clothes on as he did without.

"Thank you," finally finding my voice box.

"I figured you got held up at the salon and didn't want to bother blowing you up. I knew you'd show up so I ordered us a bottle of Merlot."

"A bottle, huh? You don't have to go all out for me. This is just a casual date. Nothing serious, you know," I leveled. He didn't respond; he just stared at me with his cat eyes and I all of the sudden started feeling self-conscious like he was trying to read me. So I reached over and placed my hand on his inner thigh, just a few inches away from Mr. Mandingo. He glanced down at my hand, took it into his and brought it up to his lips to kiss the back of it. Instinctually I pulled my hand back into my lap.

"What are you afraid of?"

"What? I'm not afraid of anything," I said defensively.

"Do you realize in the four months that we've been dealing, you have never looked me directly in the eyes? We hardly ever have decent conversations. The only time we kiss is when we're fucking and you never stay over afterwards. Why is that? What are you afraid of?"

Who the hell does this guy think he is? I knew this shit was a mistake. I ain't afraid of shit. This is what I get for listening to my lame ass friends. Now, I could choose to handle this situation in one of two ways; either reason with him and explain myself or chew him a new asshole for stepping to me sideways.

"Well, Mr. Francois, I never look you directly in the eyes because I like you better when you're banging it out behind me. We never have decent conversations because if I wanted to talk I would just find a gay guy. I never been much of a kisser and as far as staying over... the fact that you don't make enough money to afford to stay on your own should be a dead giveaway."

"Ouch. That was a little uncalled for, don't you think? You've never asked or took the time to listen to why I'm in the situation I'm in, have you?"

"Yes I have. It's the government's, your mama's, your daddy's, and the mailman's fault. I heard you loud and clear."

"You're an asshole, you know that," he said, looking pretty hurt.

"Yea and you're a loser. So I guess we're even now."

"You know, its women like you that force good men like me to step outside of ourselves and want to beat the living shit out of them," he said as he stood up, making my heart stop as I thought he was about to come through with his threat. "But my mother raised me well, so I'm just going to leave. Have a nice life Ms. Fontain," he said as he threw his money on the table and walked out of the restaurant. When he was out of sight, I picked up the folded bills and saw that he had dropped five hundred dollars on the table. In spite of all that just went down, all I could think of was the fact that I was probably holding all of his rent money in my hand. I paid the waitress for the bottle and pocketed the rest of the money. No need in crying over spilled milk; or in this case, money.

For the rest of the night I tried lining up a real date with one of my other BAMs but to my unfortunate surprise, none of them were available. My ball player from the Wizards was out of town; my chef was busy with his client's dinner party; and of course it was my doctor's night to run the ER. Things were looking real shabby for me and I was not used to that. So I decided to call one of the stylists that worked in my salon to see if she wanted to go out. I wouldn't necessarily consider her a friend but she definitely was a party partner. Plus she knew where to find all the money men; so she stayed in my good grace.

"Hey girl," she said into the receiver.

"What's up, Taneka? What are you getting into tonight?"

"Girl, you know me. I'm heading down to Skyy tonight. Ray Lewis is having his birthday bash tonight and all the Ravens are supposed to be there. I got exclusive VIP from my boo on the team so you know I'm in there like a thong on a fat chick," she laughed.

"Girl you crazy. You know you gotta get a sista in with you, right?" I asked casually as I didn't want to come off begging but I was desperate for some good entertainment, and kicking it with big burly NFL players would set me right.

"You know I got you boss lady. You're my roll dog. Be ready by eleven thirty."

"Bet. See you girl."

"Hey wait. I thought you said you had a date tonight?" she asked

"Yea I did but that scrub was a waste of time so I left," I said, stretching the truth a bit.

"You left him hi and dry? Or should I say hard and blue balled?" she cackled.

"You know me. *'No, I don't want no scrub. A scrub is a guy who can't get no love from me,'*" I sang into the phone as she joined in with singing the best song ever made by the group, TLC. "Alright girl, let me go and get ready. I think I still have enough time to run to the mall and pick me up something real quick."

"I know that's right cause we the baddest bitches in B-more and we stay fresh. Call me or text when you're ready, I'll come pick you up."

When we pulled up to the valet at the night lounge in Taneka's freshly washed white on white Range Rover, necks were twisting to try and see who we were. The women were hating of course; mainly cause they were standing in line being spectators and we were being escorted right through to the VIP section. And not the VIP that you stand in line and pay for but the VIP section that you actually have to be on the list to get into and the list is by invite only. Once we were given the wrist bands to enter the exclusive VIP section, the atmosphere changed immediately. The main party area was very club-like with people wall to wall grinding on each other. The bar area was crowded with people shouting their orders to the bartenders over the loud music. There were small sectionals placed here and there which were all over occupied by girls who looked disappointed that they were among the general population and not headed to the VIP with the real partiers. The VIP; however, took on a much more intimate appeal. There were plush white leather couches all along the wall and down the center of the room. Sheer curtains aligned the walls and pillars. Instead of a crowded bar area, there were cocktail waitresses walking around serving drinks and handing out hors devours. Even the music was different. It was a little lower so it made it easier to converse and it wasn't just booty popping music, it was more laid back but still party worthy. And of course the celebrity presence was on full blast. Not only were the Ravens players in the place but a few known rappers and actors were present. It wasn't long before Taneka and I had found ourselves in conversations with, no doubt, our next BAMs.

I was getting to know Jazz, the newest artist signed to Rep Money Records; the hottest rap label, when I felt someone staring at me from across the room. I turned to see who the gawker was and almost fell backwards once my brain registered that it was Maurice.

"What the fuck is he doing in here?" I whispered under my breath.

"Damn, you done with me already, ma?" Jazz said in his thick Brooklyn accent, trying to get my attention back.

"Oh no, sorry. Thought I saw someone I knew," I said.

"Oh, your man?"

"Baby doll, please. I don't do those."

"Man, I like you," he laughed.

"What's there not to like," I joked back, trying to avoid the death stare that I felt coming from behind me. How the hell did he manage to get in here? I was starting to get annoyed just knowing that that scrub was nearby and knowing that any minute his lame ass would be coming up to me with his 'I'm sorry and I was tripping' confessions. I made some more small talk with Jazz before moving on to work the remainder of the room. Mainly to lose sight of that clown Maurice. I found Taneka in deep conversation with her football boo and decided to leave her to her business. As I looked around, I soon realized that all the men were either already boo'd up with a chick or huddled together, probably talking about the latest game upsets. Normally I wouldn't let that deter me but I just wasn't in the mood for pretending to give a flying fuck about how many yards or touchdowns or whatever they scored. I found an empty stool in the corner and propped myself there. I figured I would just sit still and let them come to me.

After an hour of sitting by myself, babysitting a watered down Martini; I was pissed and ready to go. I couldn't believe not one guy, or girl for that matter, approached me. I wasn't used to that. They're normally lined up to talk to me. And to add insult to injury, not only did Maurice not approach me as I expected but he paid be no mind. I was starting to think that he put some Haitian voodoo hex on me. I was having the worse day ever and there didn't seem to be any ray of sunshine in sight. Just as I was about to get up and let Taneka know that I was ready to go, I spotted Maurice coming my way. Guess I spoke too soon. I tried to find a place to hide but he had already seen me and while I didn't want him in my presence, I wasn't going to look like an idiot by hall assing out the door. I stood up with my hands on my hips, ready to give him a piece of my mind for walking out on me. But instead of groveling at my feet like expected, he just walked right passed me without even looking in my direction. In fact, I don't even think he knew I was standing there. I stood there dumbfounded for a few beats. What the hell was going on tonight? I scanned the room for Taneka and found her in the same place she was an hour ago.

"Girl, I'm about to go," I said in her ear once I approached her.

"What? Go where? What's wrong?" she asked.

"I got a ride. I ran into that scrub and he begged me to go home with him," I lied.

"Girl, well get you some and then leave that chump alone," she said.

"Alright girl. I'll see you tomorrow."

"Let me know how it went."

"I will," I screamed over my shoulder. I ran through the club and out the door, hoping he was still around. I have no idea what came over me but I knew he knew I was there and the mere fact that he pretended like he didn't care irritated the hell out of me and I wanted him to know it. Once I caught up to him, he was standing at the valet booth handing the attendant his card to retrieve his car. I never understood why people with messed up cars used valet. I mean, you might as well put on a parade to people showcasing how broke you are. When I walked up behind him, that was the first thing I wanted to say but I stopped short as I surveyed him from behind. He had obviously changed from earlier. This time in slacks that fit him perfectly and a cool midnight blue shirt that seemed to make his dark skin even darker. His Stacy Adams were replaced with wing tip alligator shoes, which I know for a fact cannot be found in your local Macy's. As if I weren't already confused, the valet guy pulled in front of him in a Mercedes Benz S series. When the valet attendant handed Maurice the keys, I figured then was the time to let him have it.

"Whose car did you steal?" I teased. At first he smiled and looked in my direction but quickly erased the smile off his face once he recognized that the voice belonged to me. Instead of responding, he got in the car and shut the door. In disbelief that this guy had some huge balls to disregard me like this, I opened the passenger side and hopped in.

"Have you lost your mind? Get out of my car," he nearly screamed at me.

"Your car? Yea right. You can't afford a car like this," I said laughing as I looked around the car. There was a briefcase and scattered papers in the back and an open soda can in the cup holder.

"Do you get off on trying to make people feel like shit? Is this how you get through the day?" he said, staring at me.

"No, I just speak the truth. I'm an honest woman. I say what most are afraid to," I said still surveying the car. I noticed the headrests all had the letters "MF" monogramed on them. "Maurice Francois," I said under my breath. "How can you afford this car?"

"Get out of my car Qiana," he said as he faced forward and shifted the gears in preparation to leave.

"Can you give me a ride?"

"What? You're sitting here insulting me in my vehicle and yet you're asking me for a favor?"

"Well can you? You know you want to," I smiled at him. He glanced over at me as if he were contemplating it.

"Can I ask you a question first?"

"Oh boy," I said rolling my eyes, "go ahead."

"What's more important to you; how much money a man makes or how well he takes care of you?"

"Are you serious? In order to take care of me, a man has to make a certain amount of money. How can you take care of me if you're broke?"

"Get out," he said, reaching across me and opening my door.

"Whatever, you scrub. I don't even know why I wasted my time talking to you. I knew there was a reason I never liked talking to you. You're stupid. You have no idea what you're passing up. You'll never find pussy as good as mine in your life and you should consider yourself lucky you had a chance with this one," I said as I hopped out of the car.

"Pussy comes a dime a dozen. Holla at me when you get a brain and not just giving it," he said as he peeled off.

Fuck him. Scrub… but how did he get that car?

The next two days I was still unsuccessful in lining up a date or late night rendezvous with any of my BAMs. It was as if they were all in on this whole Sex Club activity and they weren't trying to give me none on purpose. If this was what it's like to be a virgin again, I'd much rather shoot myself. I was walking around the salon screaming and yelling at everyone over everything. I was going through penis withdrawal and I needed my fix. Truth be told, I tried to keep my sex guys to only one at a time and unfortunately for me that one was Maurice. Before Maurice it was my chef guy but he was out of town too much so I had to find a fill in. I hadn't heard from or seen Maurice since the party and I found myself thinking about him periodically. No man had ever spoken to me in the way he did and it irritated me. He needed me more than I needed him so I couldn't understand why he was being such an asshole. Ordinarily he would be blowing my phone up asking to see me. I just wanted the week to be over. I was honestly convinced that I was jinxed. By Sunday, all I wanted to do was lay in bed.

When my phone rang, I sprinted across the room to grab it out my purse before it went to voicemail. I almost threw it across the room once I saw that it was only Taneka calling.

"Whats up?" I said, clearly disappointed.

"Damn Qee, I'm happy to hear from you too."

"Sorry girl. I've just been laying in bed all day. What's up," I said, trying to sound more pleasant.

"You will never guess what my football boo just told me," she said almost squealing into the receiver.

"What?" I said, not really caring.

"When was the last time you spoke with your scrub?"

"The night of the party, why?" I asked, perking up at the mention of him. I had no idea why I was so affected by this man.

"And his full name is Maurice Francois from Haiti, right?"

I hadn't told her his full name nor had I told her his nationality so needless to say, I was fully awake. "How did you know all of that?"

"Well cause my boo is from Haiti and said that the Haitian government has contracted with this big construction company to help rebuild the country from the effects of the earthquakes. The owner of the company just passed away six months ago and now the company and this multi-million dollar contract with the Haitian government has been passed down to the owner's next of kin; his son, a one Maurice Francois of Baltimore, Maryland. Apparently all of these construction jobs that you said he's been taking was so that he can get familiar with working on a construction site because he doesn't just want to delegate, he actually plans to move back to Haiti and help with the rebuilding process." I sat on the edge of my bed staring in disbelief at what I was hearing.

"How did he find out all of this? They don't even know each other," I said, not wanting to believe that the guy I'd been calling a scrub just might be a multi-millionaire. But why wouldn't he just tell me so that I would stop calling him broke? How come he never defended his pockets?

"Here's the thing, they do know each other. Maurice apparently has always been well off but wanted to come to America to make his own money and he and my boo have been best friends since they were kids so he's always inviting Maurice to celebrity events. Hence how you initially met him. He and I were talking this morning and he was telling me about how his best friend is about to move back to Haiti and how he doesn't want him to go and so on and so on. Once I told him that I knew him, the flood gates opened and he spilled the beans."

"If that's true, why does he stay in a garden apartment with a roommate?" I said still trying to make sense of everything.

"Cause like I said, he wanted to make his own living. He didn't want to use his father's money for anything. But now that the company is his, it's his money. And his first gift to himself was to buy that brand new Benz you saw him driving in and he also gave his roommate money for a down payment to buy a condo once he leaves. He's also started a foundation for disaster relief for the people of Haiti along with his rebuilding projects. Apparently this dude is one of the good ones, girl. And word is that he's been talking about you; saying how he's met this gorgeous girl who he enjoys spending time with and want to explore something more serious with her if she'll allow him to. He even slipped up and used the "L" word but my boo said he tried to cover it up. So I suggest you give him a shout before he skips town and let him take you out and shower you with gifts."

I suddenly felt sick to my stomach. I had no idea he felt that way towards me. We hardly had a relationship or even communicated feelings for each other but he was going around raving about me. What did he see in me? Here I was, chastising a man for what he may or may not have in his pockets, all the while he was dealing with the loss of a parent and the gain of an entire country. It became very clear to me how shallow I was and yet he was still interested in me. In spite of my attitude towards him, he still accepted me and wanted to pursue something with me. And the mere fact that my friend on the other end of the phone was continuing to cosign my shallowness in spite all she just said further reflected my behavior. I wasn't always like that though. But through heartaches and headaches, I learned to form a barrier and keep men at a distance that was safe enough for me to deal with them without getting emotionally involved. It was easier to manage my heart that way. My heart; hadn't mentioned that organ in years. During our date, he had asked me what I was scared of. Well, let the truth be told, I was scared of love. I was scared of actually falling for a guy. The last time I did that, I got my head bashed into the ground and my virginity taken from my body. Playing the field had always worked for me because I put myself in a position of power with these men. No longer would I be caught off guard with my wall down. No longer would I allow someone to side swipe me with false promises of tenderness and eternal love. I let them know from the gate that all they were good for were material things and sex because that's all they've ever been good for and it always seemed to make them want me more. But this time it didn't work out that way. This time, my antics pushed him away. And it just may have come back to bite me in the ass. I hung up with Taneka and hit my speed dial to attempt to reconcile with Maurice. I never in my life had to apologize to a man so I had no idea what I was going to say but I wanted to try and see if maybe he would be willing to at least hear me out.

After a day and half of calling and texting with no response, I came to the realization that he wasn't willing to hear from me. Taneka said that he planned to head back to Haiti the end of the month, which was only two weeks away. I didn't want him to go without knowing if I could possibly open up with him and allow him to be more than any man has ever been to me. Sharon said the point of my

Sex Club activity was to go back to the basics of what a relationship is about. Not money, not sex, but love and substance. All these thoughts were running through my mind as I was driving aimlessly through the city. Often times when I have to clear my mind, I will take a drive to nowhere until my problem is resolved. Once I started seeing familiar street signs and houses, I realized that I had unintentionally driven to his apartment. Before I could put my car in reverse and high tail it out of there, he appeared from his apartment building. He was dressed in jeans and a wife beater, showing his muscular arms and I immediately got horny. Damn it had been over a week since I last had some of him and I was seriously contemplating saying fuck all this feeling shit and just ride him until I fall asleep. But then he did something that I've rarely seen him do since we've been creeping; he smiled. He had the perfect set of white teeth that seemed to sparkle in the sun. When I followed his eye sight to see what he was smiling at, I saw that it was a female walking his way. Now I've never been a jealous woman; I've never had to be because I've never cared enough. So I don't know what came over me but as soon as he and the woman embraced in a tight hug, I jumped out of the car and sped walked in their direction. She spotted me before he did and I guess she whispered to him that some deranged woman was coming their way because he whipped around with just as puzzled of a look on his face as she had.

"Qiana?" he said, probably wondering why I was in his neck of the woods unannounced. I was wondering what the hell I was doing there too but my feet seemed to be moving faster than my brain.

"So is this why you haven't been answering my phone calls or text?" I asked him as I pointed to the stick figure that was still in his arms.

"Excuse me?" he questioned, still confused at my presence.

"This?! Is this why you've been acting like you don't know me?" I yelled.

"This?! Who you think you talking to," the stick figure stepped in my face and he had the nerve to step in front of her.

"Mia, just go inside. I'll handle her. I'm sorry," he said, trying to console her as she stared me down.

"Yea, go inside *Mia* before you become M-I-A!" I yelled after her as she walked away cursing me out in what sounded like French. "Yea, yea, your mama!"

"Hey, watch your fucking mouth! That's my sister! So you talking about MY mama!" he screamed at me. I let what he said sink in before I realized that the woman I thought was his new love interest was in fact his sister. This apology thing was going to become my new best friend.

"I'm so sorry, Maurice. I didn't know," I said trying to reach for his hand but he pulled it away.

"What are you doing here?" he snapped, obviously not letting me off that easy.

"I didn't show up on purpose. I was just driving to try and clear my head and I found myself here."

"You found yourself here?" he asked in disbelief as if to say, "yea right".

"Yes and I saw you and her and I thought,"

"She was my girl," he said, finishing my sentence.

"I'm an asshole."

"Yes you are."

"Can we talk? Please?"

"What do you possibly have to say to me? I think I've heard enough of your insults and seen how much of a bitch you are to last me a lifetime. I don't think I need to indulge in anymore from you," he said as he turned and walked away.

"I don't want you to move back to Haiti." That stopped him dead in his tracks.

"What did you say?" he said as he turned back towards me.

"I said I don't want you to move back."

"How do you know I'm moving back?"

"Small world," I shrugged.

"You fucking my best friend?!" he accused, stepping back in my face.

"What? Huh? No! I don't even know who your best friend is!"

"So how the hell did you know that?!" he said taking another step in my face.

"Maybe because I'm friends with the girl he *is* fucking."

"What the fuck he tell her for?!"

"Look, I don't know. That's not the point. The point is I don't want you to go. I want you to stay here and maybe we can try to get to know each other… without sex," I said with a straight face. Couldn't believe these words were coming out of my mouth. Apparently, neither could he because he burst out laughing when I said that.

"You're a funny chick, you know that? You, not have sex? Yea right," he continued to laugh in my face.

"Yes, I would like to try and get to know you. Actually spend time with you outside the bedroom."

"Why? Cause you heard I came up on some money and I'm not this broke ass nigga like you thought I was. Cause you figured I could take care of you now that I've got money? Before when you thought I was broke, you didn't want anything from me but my dick but now that you've heard from the grapevine that papa got a brand new bag, now you trying to trade yours in?"

"No, it has nothing to do with the money," I tried to defend myself but he laughed again.

"Whatever, Qiana. Just four days ago, I straight out asked you what you thought was more important, how much a man made or how well he could take care of you and your gold digging ass said, the money. Did you not?"

"Yea I know but,"

"But what? Now you're trying to redeem yourself cause you realized that you spoke too soon? And you know what the sad thing is? I was really feeling you. I knew all of this about you. That you were a superficial woman but I thought that if I showed you that I was an honest man out here trying to make a name for myself, then you would open your eyes and see passed all the bullshit that you were used to. I could have told you about my father's company months ago but I wanted to test and see if you had the ability to see past materialistic things and get to know the man I am. I know somewhere deep down, you have a heart and one day you'll wake the fuck up and realize that you'll never heal your heart with your pussy. You're a gorgeous woman but I'm deeper than that and I need someone in my life that'll match that depth. And I'm sorry my love, but you just aren't her. I do want the best for you and I hope you wake up before it's too late cause you can't be a dick rider at fifty," he said as he leaned in and kissed me on the cheek before turning to walk away. I stood there and watched as he disappeared into his building. It's amazing how a week without sex revealed so much of me to me. It seemed like as soon as I took away my security blanket, I was faced with a huge void.

As I walked back towards my car, my phone vibrated in my pocket. When I took it out and read the caller ID, it read back; CHEF. I glanced behind me in hopes that Maurice would be standing there. When he wasn't, I whispered to myself, "Well, another one bites the dust." I wiped the tear that had escaped from my eye and pressed the green button on my phone to answer the incoming call.

"Hey baby, what are you doing tonight?"

Sharon AKA The Slave

So my friends think they can flip the script on me. I should have known that their role for me would be something like a slave or servant since they are always getting on me about my bossy ways. Especially towards men. But as the only child and owner of my own business, it's all I know. And I wouldn't necessarily call it being bossy; I just have always been a leader and sure of what I wanted out of life. I've always been the one to step up and speak first. People make it seem as though a woman is only supposed to be meek and mild and if she steps out of line she is chastised and called a bitch. I never understood that. We are the bearers of life; shouldn't it be natural that we then lead it? Shouldn't we be able to put men in their place and guide them in the direction that we want them to go? That's what they do with us. The POWER of the P should take us further than the bedroom. I just think women are too afraid to take charge out of fear of being alone. But ironically, more men try to pursue me because they see me as a challenge than they do some of my less confident friends. The fact that my friends wanted me to play the role of a slave further goes to show the reluctance of women to accept the notion that we have been slaves already and that maybe they should consider a new way of thinking. But I digress. The Sex Club was my idea and therefore I will go along with the role they have given me JUST to prove the redundancy of it.

Like clockwork, my phone rang and without looking to see who it was, I answered, "Hey Craig."

"Evening Sharon, are you available to speak right now?"

"I keep telling you my dear, if I answer the phone, I can talk. You don't have to ask me every time you call me."

Craig is not normally the kind of man I would date. He is what some would call a certified geek. He creates video games for a living and quite frankly, I'm still flabbergasted on how that is even a legit career. I met him at a promotional event I was attending for a new client of mine. We literally collided into each other trying to rush to our respected events. When he scrambled onto the floor trying to retrieve all of the papers that went flying out of my briefcase, I couldn't help but to check him out. From head to toe, he was totally not the kind of man that I would look twice at. From his small afro atop his head to his suspenders and over worn loafers, the man was all kinds of wrong. And yes, you heard me right, he wore suspenders. I was ready to push passed him as he handed me my papers but I got a good look at his face and I froze. The man was beyond handsome. His skin was so clear that it looked like he wore makeup, which was rare in a fair skin African American person. His high cheek bones and squared chin gave him a very masculine and dominating appeal, which was an obvious contradiction to his attire and demeanor. Even the dimple in his chin seemed to be meant for a carpenter or model and not for a man who had the audacity to step out in public with suspenders on. So I'm sure you're wondering how a woman of my stature ended up dating a man who probably didn't own a mirror. Well long story short; he apologized profusely and insisted on taking me out to lunch to make up for his carelessness. I was impressed with his forwardness and after giving his face another once over and trying my hardest to not let my gaze go beyond that, I agreed. There would be no harm in letting him take me to lunch. So I told him when and where to meet me and ensured that I pay for my own meal; didn't want him thinking that we would be starting anything together. But our lunch turned out really well, besides some obvious differences, we actually had a lot in common. In spite of his choice of clothing and profession, he was a pretty normal guy. A tad bit passive but normal nonetheless. Maybe that's why I like him, because he allows me to make decisions and he just goes along with it. I know that sounds bad but it really works for us. He knows what he wants and has no problem with voicing it, so for the most part; he just takes the back seat and lets me drive. So that's another reason why this week's Sex Club activity was going to be a challenge for both of us because we both are comfortable in our roles in the relationship.

"You're correct. I just like to always make sure I'm not being of a disturbance to you," he said.

"I understand. So what's up?"

"Just got finished my layout project and now I'm waiting for my Queen to let me know what she wants to do tonight."

Did I mention that this is by far the best relationship I've ever been in? He's totally into me and about making me happy. After almost a year of being together, I can't recall ever having a serious argument. So again, I'm not sure how this week was going to pan out for us. But I figured I had to oblige.

"You know Craig, let's do something that you want to do tonight," I heard myself say.

"Really?!" he said as if his lifelong dream had just come true.

"Well goodness, don't sound so much like a kid being let off of punishment," I said, a bit taken aback by his excitement; as if he was holding that in for a long time.

"It's not that, it's just there's this new Warcraft Tournament going on and I REALLY wanted to go to it but I figured you wouldn't in a million years agree to it," he said. Got that right! Why did he have to be so corny and sexy all at the same time?

"You're a slave, Sharon. Whatever he says, whatever he wants," I whispered to myself.

"I'm sorry?"

"Oh, I said, 'Of course I'll go'. Whatever you want to do tonight, I'm down," I said through clenched teeth.

"Super! I'll go get dressed and pick you up in an hour," he said, hanging up without even waiting for a response or saying good bye.

Did he just say, 'Super'?

We arrived at the tournament and it took everything in my powers not to bolt out the door. The entire place was swarming with kids and adults who looked to be on the verge of pedophilia. Craig clenched my hand as he took me around to the different booths of competitions that were going on.

"So are you going to play?" I asked, hoping to God above that he would say no.

"Oh no, no. I play all day at work. This is merely research. Just to see how everyone is enjoying my creation," he boasted.

"You created this one?" I asked in surprise. In the year of dating him, I rarely asked him about exactly what it is he did. I knew he was an animator for video games but I just figured he helped out, never knew he actually was the mastermind behind a game that hundreds of people were lined up to compete in.

"Sure did. Who would have thunk it? A black kid from Chicago would grow up to create one of the country's bestselling video games? Guess it's not so bad being a geek after all, huh?" he beamed as we continued to walk hand in hand around the packed arena.

I guess this whole time I had been underestimating him. His skills and smarts were incredible. I had no idea what it took to design or create a video game but just from the looks of things, I was blown away. I remember as a kid, Super Mario Bros and Pac Man were as complex as our video games got. But this game, as gruesome and grueling as it was, I was astonished at how real it looked. I felt like I was watching a movie instead of a video game. I guess my mouth being hung open was a dead giveaway to him that I was impressed so for the rest of the night he broke down to me as much as I could comprehend, how what I was looking at in front of me came to be.

I must say that I gained a new found respect for Craig by the end of the night. He wasn't just some nerdy guy; he actually was really gifted, genius maybe. Listening to him talk about a passion of his, I witnessed something in him for the first time; emotion. He talked about his work as if it were a child of his; the dedication and care that he put into it shown all over his face. But what impressed me the most about him was his humbleness about his work. Here he is the guy who made this incredible game and yet he didn't want anyone to know. He could have easily let the people who checked us in know who he was and we could have gotten the royal treatment but he didn't. He chose to mingle and blend in with the crowd. He wasn't in it for the fame and recognition; he just really enjoyed what he did.

"Why are you so quiet," he asked me as we drove back to his place from the event.

"I'm just thinking," I said, staring out the window.

"Care to share?"

I glanced over at his smiling face and frowned. "Why are you with me?" I blurted out.

"Pardon?"

"Why are you with me? I mean, we've been together for almost a year and I feel like this whole time it's been about me. I've been a selfish bitch to you and yet you're still here... smiling," I said, sincerely.

"Oh, I wouldn't say all of that. I know you're a bit controlling but that's what makes you happy and it's my job to keep you happy so I have no problem with it," he assured.

"Well that's not a good thing. What about you, though? What about your wants and needs? If it's always about me, when do you get satisfied?"

"When you do. When I'm with someone, it's not about me, it's about her. When she's happy, so am I. I believe that in a relationship, if everyone cared for and catered to the other, then no one is left out but when you only think of self, someone is always left in the cold."

"Well guess you're frost bitten then," I said, ashamed to admit that he was right. He laughed at my comment and reached over and grabbed my hand. After seeing a side of him tonight that I had never witnessed, it had dawned on me that I had been selfish in this relationship. I was relishing in the fact that here was a man that would answer my every beckoning call but what I failed to realize is that, here was a man. A man who had needs and wants himself and if I was going to be with him, it was my job to fulfill them. Maybe I had been using him this whole time but not because I was malicious but because he conformed to my ways. It started to become clear to me that maybe my friends were onto something with this whole slave activity. I think Craig deserved to be catered to for a change.

"So, my King, what would you like to do next?" I asked as I brought his hands up to my lips and kissed them.

"Your King? You've never called me that before," he blushed.

"Well I want tonight to be about you and if I'm your Queen, then it's only fit that you be my King, correct?"

"Yea, I, I guess so," he stuttered.

"So? What would you like to do next?" I repeated.

"I was just going to ask you what you wanted to do because it doesn't matter to me," he said, alittle uneasy.

I knew this wasn't going to be easy. He wasn't just going to outwardly start taking over things. I would have to let him in on the activity without letting him know that it was an activity.

"How about this? Lets try something new. Like a game. How about for the next week, we switch positions. You be the controlling one and I follow. Whatever you want to do, we'll do. You make all the decisions and I'll go along," I suggested.

"But why? I'm not controlling. It's not in me to be," he contested.

"Yes I know but I feel like we have no balance. I want to cater to you for a change and I want you to learn to loosen up and speak up more about what you want. You just said that if each partner is about the other then no one is left out, well you've been all about me for ten months, I think you deserve some 'me' time for a week," I said, looking him square in the face. "Anything you want to say, do, ask, feel, express, you have free reign to do so. You don't have to ask me, just make the decision. Starting tonight."

"Tonight?"

"Tonight."

"Well there's this one thing that I've wanted to do for the longest with you but I figured you would think I was crazy or a freak," he said.

"Nope, no judgment from me. I trust you," I said sincerely.

"Well… when I was creating Warcraft, I wanted to put in a sex scene between two of the characters to help with the storyline but I'm the kind of creator that has to actually see my ideas in action and not just in my head in order for me to approve the concept. This was really early on in our relationship and I just knew that you wouldn't agree to it."

I suddenly became uneasy. Maybe I had spoken too soon. Craig and mine's sex life was good. He knew exactly what to do with the equipment that God had blessed him with but just like every aspect in our relationship, he allowed me to lead and he graciously followed. "Are you asking me to do a sex scene in your video game?!" I nearly screamed, almost scaring him.

"No, that's not what I'm asking you. Never mind. I knew I shouldn't have opened my mouth. I'm sorry, Sharon, I didn't mean to offend you."

"No, you didn't offend me. I apologize. I cut you off. Continue, please," I assured him by placing my hand on his leg.

"I would never subject you to something like that. Besides, the characters aren't real, its animation," he said with a bit of attitude in his voice which oddly turned me on. He had real conviction when it came to these video games, I see.

"I know dear, I apologize. I'm listening."

"I just wanted to know if maybe you would like to role play. In the privacy of my house, no cameras or anything like that."

"Sure, whatever you like," I said quickly before I could change my mind.

"Really?" he said shocked that I responded so quickly. "Role playing the characters from the game?"

"Is this just for enjoyment or are you researching?"

"Oh it's definitely enjoyment. The game is already finished," he said with the biggest grin on his face.

"Then sure, if it'll make you happy."

He placed my hand on top of the bulge that was forming in his pants. "Is this happy enough?"

When we got to his house, he told me to wait in the living room while he 'set up the scene'. He practically sprinted through his apartment, knocking things over as he set up. It was almost comical how happy he was to have one of his obvious fantasies come true. I would just have to try my hardest not to laugh. Twenty minutes had passed before I heard my name being called from his room.

"Sharon, go to the guest bathroom where you'll find your costume and storyline," he said from behind his closed bedroom door. "Let me know when you're ready."

My costume?! What the hell was this man up to? He couldn't be serious. When I opened the bathroom door, I saw that he was. There was a Zena Warrior Princess-like costume hanging up behind the door, complete with gladiator sandals. I tried to turn on the lights but he had taped the light switch down to keep the lights off. The only light available was from four small candles on top of the toilet that were lit.

"Umm, Craig, I need the lights and you've seemed to prevent that from happening," I yelled from the bathroom.

"Read the storyline," he yelled back.

"Well I need light in order to read!" I waited for a response and when none came, I picked up the paper that was taped to the front of the costume and held it to one of the candles and read:

You are Trea, a woman living in the jungles of Indonesia. Your tribe has been demolished by a raging war and you will stop at nothing to defend what's left of it. I am Buzz, a captain of the US Marines whose airplane has crash landed in the middle of your tribe. I come in peace but in your eyes, I am the enemy. All you know to do now is to fight to defend and avenge your father's death. You try to attack and kill me, thinking I am the enemy but my military training and strength over powers you and I'm able to subdue you. Together we are able to overcome our differences and take on the enemies united as one.

What the fuck?! He can NOT be serious! There is no way in the world I am going to play dress up and actually fight him! How is this his sexual fantasy?

"Craig, I'm sorry honey but I can't do this," I said as I opened the door, prepared to give him the bad news. My eyes met blackness as he had turned out all of the lights in the house and had jungle sounds playing from his surround sound that was planted in his walls throughout the apartment. This is what I get for listening to my friends. No, this is what I get for trying to meddle in their love lives because had I not, they would have never come up with this activity and I would not be in this predicament. I slammed the door and sat on the floor. I knew I had two choices; I could barge into his room and demand he come back to the real world or I could suck it up for one night and play along; for him. I took a deep breath and looked up at the horrific costume that seemed to be mocking me and decided that I would just go along with this dumb fantasy and pray that it wasn't too painful.

I squeezed my body into the very revealing and snug costume that seemed to be torn and tattered purposely along the breast and butt areas. Good thing I worked out that morning because other than a top that barely covered my breasts and a skirt that left nothing to the imagination, I was naked. What tribe was this girl from? The lady of the night Tribe?

"Ok Craig, I'm ready. I guess," I yelled as I opened the door to the darkness once again. When no response came, I became a bit agitated. "I said I'm ready. Where are you?" I stood in place listening for him but all I could hear were the stupid birds and frogs coming from his soundtrack. "Ok, this isn't funny. Say something," I yelled, trying to reach for light switches. I found another taped one and ripped the tape off and flicked the switch but to my dismay, nothing happened. As I was about to turn and make my way back into the bathroom, I heard a loud boom the literally shook the walls. I screamed and fell to the ground with my ass in the air. "Craig, are you crazy?! I don't want to play anymore! Come out now! Isn't there a safe word or something? Olli olli oxen free or something like that?" I low crawled back to what I thought was the bathroom but was met by more darkness. There were no candles in sight just blackness. I noticed that in the bathroom he had covered the window with a dark, thick drapery and I was starting to think that's what he had done to every window in the house because my eyes had yet to adjust to the dark. As I was about to stand up and scream out again, this time about how I would call the police if he didn't come out, an arm grabbed me hard by the waist and pushed me up against the wall. Startled, my first reaction was to swing. For a second I had forgotten that I was in a make believe situation and started fighting for my life. I started kicking and screaming for the imposter to let me go. But he pushed his body up against mine and pinned my arms to the wall. I kept screaming and squirming in spite of his weight on me. I felt him lean into my ear. "Calm down, I'm not going to hurt you," he said in the most deep and sexy tone. I immediately stopped squirming as my nipples began to harden from feeling his breath on my neck. I came back to reality and realized that the voice was coming from Craig. I had never heard his voice so deep nor had I ever known him to be so strong.

"Let me go, Craig," I pleaded, halfway hoping that he wouldn't.

"Name's Buzz," he said leaning closer into my neck, slightly grazing it with his nose. "And you need to calm down missy. I'm not your enemy, I come in peace," he said as he planted a feather light kiss on my neck that sent chills down my spine.

"Let me go," I whispered again.

"Not until you calm down. You damn near took my head off and we can't have that. I'm sure you've already seen enough of that," he said as he planted another kiss under my chin.

"Well, what do you want from me?" I asked out of nowhere.

"I want to join forces with you so that we can put an end to this madness and get you your tribe back," he said, nibbling on my chin. I was getting heated and my breathing was becoming labored as I could feel the excitement rising between his legs.

"And how exactly do we join forces," I breathed as he took my bottom lip into his and suckled on it.

"Let me show you," he said as he picked me up and carried me further into the dark room. He flicked on a lamp and the red bulb partially illuminated the room. He placed me onto a blanket and stepped back and for the first time since this whole thing started, I got to see him. He had on form fitting khaki pants that were tucked into his military boots. His khaki shirt was almost too small as it hugged his arms and chest. The majority of his everyday clothing was loose fitting so this was different for him and I was liking what I saw. He wasn't very muscular but he had enough definition in his exposed abs to make my mouth water. I wanted to say something; felt like I should but my brain seemed to be asleep. He knelt down in front of me and began to kiss and lick my toes. I gasped initially as I wasn't used to my toes getting attention and wasn't prepared for the sensation that it sent through my whole body. The gentle rhythm of his soft tongue made me wet instantly. He gave each toe the same attention as if to not make the others jealous. By the tenth toe, I was clenching the blanket trying to suppress an orgasm that was trying to surface.

"Please no, stop. I can't take it," I pleaded to him.

Without missing a beat, he said, "this is for the betterment of your tribe." He then started kissing up my leg and raised it in the air so that he could lick behind my knee and a jolt of pleasure shot straight down my legs to my sex. He continued down my leg to my thighs and made his way towards the middle. I hadn't bothered to keep my panties on seeing as though I knew they would be eventually coming off, so when he put his face mere inches away from my pleasure spot, I felt my juices start to flow. He didn't dive right in like I wanted him to; instead he just lingered over me so that I could feel every breath he took. He began to lightly blow circles and I sang out in pleasure and agony as he was obviously teasing me.

"Stop teasing me, please," I begged through gasps.

"You said whatever I want, right?" he asked, still hovering over my wetness.

"Huh?"

"You said that I get whatever I want, correct?" he repeated.

"Yea, yea, that's what I said, now come on, PLEASE," I pleaded.

"Well then, no. That's not what I want," he said as he sat up and in one motion grabbed me, threw me over his shoulder and stood up.

"What the hell are you doing?"

"One thing I want is for you to shut up," he said seriously. That definitely caught me by surprise as he had never uttered those words to me before. Oddly enough, it made my rivers flow even faster. He slapped me on the ass and said as he walked us out of the room, "I see I'm going to have to show you who's the boss around here, woman. I know you have a mission to accomplish for your tribe but you won't get anywhere unless we unite together. So I suggest you just shut up and follow my lead. Obviously you haven't been able to accomplish anything on your own."

He walked us into the kitchen and laid me on top of the table. Everything was still dark but I could tell from the sound of the refrigerator that that's where we were. He spread my legs wide and sat down in the chair in front of me. The next thing I knew, I felt something cold dripping between my legs and I shuttered at the intense feeling. He began to spread the creamy stuff all over my sex with his fingers, paying special attention to my exotic bulb. I heard him place his fingers in his mouth and suck on them as if they were his favorite lollipop. He then teased my clitoris with his finger before replacing it with the tip of his tongue. He started in small circles and before long was fully sucking as if it were a pacifier. I was in heaven. I don't recall ever screaming that loud with him or any man for that matter. For what seemed like forever, he indulged in a feast that included my nectar and various products from his refrigerator. I lost count of the number of orgasms when he pulled out the ice and steam. The hot and cold combination sent my eyes rolling in the back of my head. When he finished, he stood up from the table and said, "Mission one has been accomplished; to subdue the tribal princess. Now you go and get some rest because mission two will require all of your energy." He picked me up from the table and carried me to his room and laid me on his bed. I was too worn out to protest so I rolled over and fell right to sleep.

When I woke up the next morning, I had on his pajama top and a pair of my panties that I kept in a drawer he had given me. I looked around the room and saw our costumes neatly folded on top of his arm chair in the corner. I realized that I hadn't dreamt last night. Even though there was no intercourse, that may have been the most I orgasm in one setting. Strangely, I think it was the whole setting that did it. The costumes, the jungle sounds, the barbarian antics, and his aggressiveness, oh yea, that definitely set me straight. I never knew he was that strong to pick me up and carry me as if I were a rag doll. I'm not a full figured woman but I had enough meat on my bones to add a little pressure to his medium frame.

I hopped out of the bed and went to look for my phone to call my office and let them know that I would be late. When I opened the door, I was startled and almost fell back as Craig was standing right there in the doorway. He wore nothing but the bottoms to the top I had on.

"Morning princess," he said, grinning from ear to ear.

"Morning to you too, crazy man," I said as I embraced him.

"Sleep well?" he said, kissing me on top of my head.

"I sure did. Thank you."

"Don't thank me yet," he said as he took my hand and led me into the bathroom. "Mission one was a success. Now it's time for Mission two; getting the princess cleansed so that we may unite," he said undoing the buttons on the oversized pajama top. He carefully removed my panties and helped me into the bubble filled bath tub. He then removed his pants and sat in the tub behind me. He began rubbing my back and shoulders.

"This is some fantasy of yours," I said relishing in the good feeling I was getting from his massage.

"This stopped being about a fantasy a long time ago. This is about you letting go and allowing me to take control of a situation, no matter what. No matter how crazy or obscured. If you trust me as your man, you will follow my lead. I made all that fantasy stuff up just to see if you would allow yourself the chance to really lose the control and strong hold that you've put on yourself and everything in your life, including me. I love you Sharon, almost from the beginning. I know we are an unlikely pair but I think that's what makes us work. We complement each other. You're more assertive and I'm laid back. My only wish for you is that you allow me the opportunity to assert myself more often and YOU lay back," he said as he lightly tugged on my shoulders, gesturing for me to lay back into him. "See? There you go! Not so bad now is it?" He started caressing my breasts and kissing my neck.

For the first time in a VERY long time, if ever, I relaxed. I completely let go into his chest and laid there and let him do whatever it was that he wanted without a thought or interference from me. I closed my eyes as I felt his hands begin to descend down my torso and slide between my legs. He gently inserted two fingers into my heat and I gasped at the assured expertise his fingers seemed to have. How they knew exactly where my spot was as if they were Columbus and they were discovering the center of me. He intensified his thrusts and I gripped the sides of the tub as I was close to eruption. As if he knew what was coming next, he removed his fingers and whispered in my ear, "Not yet. I want you to hold it for me. Can you do that for me?" When I nodded, he responded, "good girl. Now stand up, I want to taste your sweetness." Without hesitation or argument, I obeyed his command. He began to indulge and it took everything in my powers to not slip and fall backwards. Without another word, he stood up and lifted me up and lowered me onto his wonderful blessing and I went crazy. When I tell you that for a year, this man has held back, I am not exaggerating. We normally only do missionary or me on top. I'm not sure if it was because he was afraid to take over or if he was just allowing me to lead but THIS was NOT our norm and I was oh so loving it! If this was what it meant to let go then God please take my hands away from me because I don't ever want to hold on again, unless it's onto his shoulders as he pumps his package all the way through me. He stepped out of the tub with me still in his arms and my sugar walls still surrounding his sugar cane and sat me on the bathroom counter and continued to make love to me. We performed almost every position from the Kama Sutra in that bathroom and after two hours, we laid on the floor exhausted but grinning from ear to ear.

"Wow," was all I could muster up the strength to say.

"I know right. I'm good girl. Don't sleep on us geeks," he playfully teased.

I was amazed at how good love making could completely change a person's thought process. I started reflecting on my Sex Club activity role as the slave. I wasn't necessarily his slave but I did allow him to lead and make decisions that even in the bedroom, I would not normally have. I've never allowed a man to take control of the relationship in my life out of fear that once I let go, he will ultimately lead me to heart break. But for some reason, I trusted that Craig would lead me to happiness and not just in the bedroom but in our entire relationship. For the remainder of the week, I let him do whatever it is he wanted to do. If he wanted to watch reruns of Star Wars, then that's what we did. If he thought that the bed should be fixed a certain way, then that's how we fixed it. When he asked me to wear my hair down instead of my usual ponytail, I quickly obliged. Our relationship as a whole was never broken but this slight alteration has actually brought us closer and I feel like we actually are a lot happier. I even caught him checking out some rings in the mall when he thought I wasn't looking. Every once in awhile my controlling ways resurfaced but the beautiful thing about us is that he didn't mind. He just wanted to be able to have a say in some decisions that were made between us. And judging by the sex animal he displayed those first few days, I definitely would not object to his decisions at all!

BAGGAGE

Baggage to Die For

"The dictionary defines love as: "A profoundly tender and passionate affection for another person. A deep and enduring emotional regard towards another." Reading this definition helped to validate the feelings that had been surging through my veins. *A deep and enduring emotional regard.* That's permanent, long lasting. That kind of feeling is not something that blows through the wind; it's concrete. To further explain my current state of emotions, I went to our beloved Bible and read a passage that says: *"Love is patient, love is kind. It does not envy, it does not boast, it is not proud. It does not dishonor others, it is not self-seeking, it is not easily angered, it keeps no record of wrongs. Love does not delight in evil but rejoices with the truth. It always protects, always trusts, always hopes, always perseveres. Love never fails."* LOVE NEVER FAILS. You hear that? It NEVER fails. Not sometimes, not except on Tuesdays and not when it's convenient or when you're tired, but NEVER. Another state of permanence. Don't get me wrong, it's not that I needed these definitive words to tell me what I already knew; its just comforting to know that what I feel can be so accurately put into words for the world to see. The love I feel for you is intense. Like nothing I've ever felt for someone in my entire life. I consecrate my love to you. I know our relationship hasn't always gone smoothly but just as it said in the Bible, to love someone is to be patient and never be easily angered or keep records of wrong. And we both know, I've been wrong a lot but our love won't allow that to matter.

"I remember when we first met. It was your first week at the office and you hardly knew anyone. You looked so beautiful in your purple blouse and crisp black slacks. Impressed that I even remember what you wore, huh? I pay attention to everything that concerns you. Although strangers, your warm smile felt very welcoming to me. Being in IT, I rarely am greeted by smiles; it's normally a lot of huffing and puffing and complaining about why their network is malfunctioning. But you were different; you were pleasant and very patient as I set up your network for you. Now I have never been a very forward man but there was something about your demeanor that drew me in and made me want to know more; good thing for me your network would take a little while to get going so I took a chance and chatted you up. We talked about our backgrounds, our work experiences, what you should come to expect around the office, and even laughed about the recent gossip being spread around about the CEO and his not so secret affair with the cleaning girl. You were a real breath of fresh air to me and I knew that you were going to be a joy to work with. And I must say that in the weeks that followed, I found that to be only the tip of our growing iceberg. You always greeted me with a hello and a smile and asked me how my morning was going. We started having lunch in the cafeteria together and I always ensured that you got to your car safely at the end of the day, even when you weren't aware. It was like we were forming our own little ritual. And our first date was the sweetest date I'd ever been on. You and I both know that I've never been much of a date guy but you seemed to just bring out these suppressed desires that I never thought I had; that made me want to go to the moon with you if you asked. I really enjoyed our one on one time and got to know you on a more personal and private level. I was in awe of you already as you displayed a woman of honor and substance. And when we kissed, I know it sounds a bit far fetched and animated, but I swear I saw fireworks. Your lips felt like pillows and I'm pretty sure even with my dark skin, you could see the blush forming on my face. The next day I believe was when I was locked into my feelings towards you; when you had those flowers delivered to my office with that heartfelt thank you note attached to it. Now, I'm not quite saying that it was love at that point but it was something. Unfortunately because of our crazy schedules, we weren't able to coordinate another date but our lunch dates were more than enough for us in the meantime. Actually it was more like your busy schedule as you started making friends around the office and hanging out with them after work. I know you tried to invite me but I've never really been much of a fan of any of those guys, so I declined. I would have rather just spent those times nestled up to you but as the Bible says, "love is patient". Ha! Look at that, I said love. Maybe it was love at that time but I was just too confused to know it. It had almost been a month since our first date and a few days had gone by since you showed up for our usual lunch dates, so I started to get worried about you. I'm sure all of the stress from the new job and a new area was starting to get to you and I wanted to be the best boyfriend to you so I figured that I would purchase the best bottle of wine, some massage oils and a relaxation CD and pamper my woman after a long days work. That's all it was honey. I still don't understand why you got so mad at me. I wasn't trying to "invade your space" or be overbearing like you accused. I thought I was just doing what any man would for his woman. But when you said that you needed your space from me; I just felt like my heart dropped. Honestly, tell me. What did I do wrong? Had I not been the epitome of what a true gentleman is? Had I not put you on a pedestal like a queen deserves to be? Huh? So why then would you need space from that? And you allowed yourself to fall victim to that scum bag's lies. He's a womanizer! How could you agree to let him take you out? We could have communicated our problems better and worked on rebuilding what we had started but that jerk with his slithering conniving words swooped down in your time of weakness and preyed on you. And I don't blame you one bit. You were hurt and vulnerable and he took advantage of that. Fucking bastard! Sorry honey, excuse my language but men like that, men who come in and break up happy homes are disgusting pigs and they deserve to sleep with the fishes. Hahahaha, I heard that on a mafia movie one time and thought it sounded appropriate to insert there. But you wont have to worry about that dirt bag ever again. I took care of him for you."

"You're crazy!" she cried. "What did you do to him?!"

"Honey, you're shaking. Shhhh, don't talk. You're just going to get yourself even more upset," I assured her in my calmest voice. I definitely didn't want to upset her anymore than I already had.

"Oh my God! What is wrong with you?! Untie me! Please!!"

"Now I can't do that because if I do then you'll run and we've already been down that road today," I sincerely smiled at her, admiring her beauty. I hadn't planned on tying her up but after I realized she wouldn't sit here and listen to me without trying to run, I had to do what was necessary at the time to get her attention. After a few moments of staring at her face, I finally said, "How did a guy like me luck out and get a girl like you?"

"WHAT?! YOU ARE SICK! YOU NEVER GOT ME! These stories and this relationship that you have formed in your head is not real! Oh my God!"

"Wow. Now that really hurt. What you just said right there, that hurt. As I said before, I know we've had our problems, but what couples don't."

"WE ARE NOT AND HAVE NEVER BEEN A COUPLE!"

"So our date never meant anything? And the kiss. What about the kiss? That didn't mean anything to you," I said almost heartbroken as her deceitful words started to pierce my heart.

"Are you serious? What date? We never went out on a date! You can't be serious right now. Please don't do this to me. Don't hurt me," she cried. It pained me to see her hurt like this.

"I'm not trying to hurt you baby. That's why I brought you here, to heal both of our hearts forever."

"For, forever, oh my God. We never had a relationship. You came to my house one time to help fix my computer and I fed you. That was it."

"So you mean to tell me, you kiss every man that comes and helps you fix things at your house! Is that what you did with that pig?!" I screamed at her. I have never been an emotional man and have rarely gotten into arguments with people so being here in this state of being is even more truth that this is real. She's just scared. Scared of love.

"I kissed you on the cheek as a thank you. You took time out of your day to help me. If I would have known that you would have reacted in this way, I would have never given you the flowers. I was just being nice," she said, barely above a whisper.

"Aww and that's what I love about you honey," I said caressing her hair. "Your thoughtfulness. I love how everyday during lunch, you would always pick the table right next to the window because somehow you knew that I loved to be by a window where I could see outside. That's more than just being nice, my dear."

"Oh God, I should have listened when they warned me about you but I was just being nice. I was just letting you sit with me because… I was just being nice. I didn't know anybody and you seemed like a nice enough guy at the time and... and... and... I was just being nice," she wailed in a full out hysterical cry. I held her in my arms and let her cry. Cry for our love.

"That's it baby, let it out. This will make it all clearer for you. After today we won't have to worry about anyone ever coming in between us ever again."

"PLEASE don't hurt me. My family will be looking for me if I don't call them like I normally do. Please! If you want a date, I'll go out on a date with you. Just please don't hurt me. PLEASE! I beg you! Don't hurt me!"

I started to cry too as the love of my life's heart obviously needed mending. "Baby, I'm here for you. I'm right here. I'm not going anywhere. I'm not going to hurt you. I just want us to be together, like God promised. He made one woman from one man. Everyone has their equal, their soul mate; their other half. And we have been blessed to have found ours in each other. So we no longer need to search any more." I put my hands on each side of her face and stared at this woman that would soon be joined to me for all eternity and my heart began to beat rapidly in my chest. I couldn't wait any longer, so I said to the beautiful gift God had placed before me, *"'Bone of my bones, and flesh of my flesh: she shall be called woman because she was taken out of man.'"* I sweetly said as I planted a loving kiss on her lips and lingered there for a few moments, basking in her sweetness and flowing tears as they continued to fall from her eyes. "Now I'm just going to place this gently over your mouth so that we don't involve anyone else in our union," I said, gently placing a strip of duct tape over her mouth. She began breathing wildly and yelling through her duct tape. I wanted badly for her to stop but I told myself that no matter what, this was best and that it had to be done this way in order for God's word to become true. This is God's work! Not mine! She and I were destined. Why couldn't she see that? She was the first woman to show me that much attention and affection and I know its all because of God. You can't stop fate. You can NOT stop what God has already put into play. I leaned in and kissed her wet cheeks one more time and then stood up. I looked around the empty basement of my townhouse and surveyed everything. The candles that I had lined up all a long the floor were glowing bright and the piles of newspapers that I had been collecting for the past few weeks were strategically placed around her and me. As I picked up the gasoline container I thought to myself that maybe I should say some words to my wife as we prepared for our union with God. Pouring the gasoline onto the wood floors, I recited, "'who *can find a virtuous woman? For her price is far beyond rubies. The heart of her husband doth safely trust in her, so that he shall have no need of spoil. She will do him good and not evil ALL the days of her life.'* That is you my dear. I'm speaking of you." When I finished, the floor and newspapers were soaked in gasoline. I said a quick prayer that the gas stove upstairs had been running long enough to fill the house by now and do what we needed it to do. I sat down next to her and she was still trembling, so I wrapped my arms around her and held her tight. "I'll love you forever. Amen," I whispered in her ear as I lit the match.

Newlywed Baggage

I remember the first time it happened. It was on our honeymoon in the Bahamas. The first few days went by smoothly; she was now Mrs. Gabriel Wise and was looking as beautiful as ever. I wanted everything to be right so anything she wanted, I delivered without thought. This was my first time in years out of the country and was never one to frequent beaches but when she suggested that we lay out in the sun, I quickly gathered our beach stuff and headed for the door.

"What are you looking at?!" she snapped at me as I set up our chairs and over sized umbrella in the sand.

"Huh? I wasn't looking at anything, Chellie. I'm setting up the beach stuff so we can relax in the sun like you asked," I idly said to her over my shoulder as I struggled with keeping the umbrella upright.

"Yea right. You must think I'm stupid. I saw you peaking out of the corner of your eye at that half naked floozy," she said from behind me.

"You're tripping, Chelles. I don't know what floozy you're talking about. And besides, how could you possibly know what I'm looking at when my back is turned to you and I'm standing under this humongous umbrella?" I said, breathless as I finally won the battle between me and the beach umbrella. When I turned around to face my wife, she had her arms crossed and was glaring at me. "What? Why are you looking at me like that?"

"You must think I'm stupid. Don't you?" she said seriously.

"Stupid about what? What are you talking about?"

"You think that I'm going to stand here and let you just lie to my face like that?!" she nearly screamed at the top of her lungs at me, flailing her arms and head like a mad woman. In the year that I'd known Michelle, I'd sadly gotten used to her unpredictable temper. Believe it or not she even yelled at me on our first date. But our upbringings were very different; I, raised in a very traditional Christian home and she, in a very dysfunctional and broken one, so I came to learn that her way of showing love was by yelling and anger. It was a bit jarring at first as I'm no timid man but I have been raised to always respect and keep your head about women. Once I got to really know the woman behind all of that, I quickly fell in love; deeply and after a while, she started to calm down a bit as she realized that love did not equal fear. But every now and again, something would trigger her and she would go off into one of her shouting frenzies. So I took this to be one of those times. I figured that all of the stress from the wedding had built up and she was finally releasing it; sadly on me, the man she just promised to love and cherish until death do we part. "Are you ignoring me?!" she said, stepping into my face. I tried to put my arms around her waist but she stepped back away from my grasp. "I'm ready to go back to the room now."

"WHAT?! But we just got down here and you saw how hard it was for me to get the umbrella up. Come on babe, let's not do this on our honeymoon. Look, I know you're stressed but the wedding is over and now its time for us to just enjoy each other," I said trying to cuddle up to her again but this time she slapped my hand away and walked back towards the hotel without a word. I stood there in disbelief for a few moments as my new wife had officially made our honeymoon a nightmare. Not wanting to walk into an argument, I sat down on the beach chair and decided that since I made all the effort to set up, I might as well enjoy it, even if it's by myself. I loved my wife with all of my heart but sometimes her insecurities really messed with me because I just couldn't understand why she didn't see what I did. I prayed that one day she would and really enjoy what we had cause it's a great thing if she would just let it be.

An hour later I walked back to the resort to return the rented equipment and decided to buy Chellie a bouquet of exotic flowers from one of the merchants in front of the resort. She had commented on how beautiful they looked and I wanted to cheer her up. When I walked up to the room door, I put my ear to the door to see if she was in the room or not. I didn't hear anything so I put the key in the door and opened it. Before I could close the door and turn on the light, I felt a sharp pain on the side of my head and stumbled in surprise as one of my wife's heels had just been hurdled at me.

"What the," I managed to say but before I could utter another sound, I was hit again with another shoe; this time, hitting me right square in the eye. "OOWWW! MICHELLE?!" I screamed out in pain as that blow brought me to my knees.

"YOU THINK I'M FUCKING STUPID DON'T YOU?!" my wife appeared in my view with the craziest look on her face. She almost looked possessed. I took a quick glance around the room and I noticed that she had thrown all of my clothes onto the small balcony outside. She had managed to flip the mattress over and the table was lying on its side. Before I could regain my composure and register what was going on, I felt a swift kick to the side of my face as I hadn't been aware of how close she was standing to me. Completely unguarded, I toppled over onto my side as my entire face felt like it was on fire. "SO YOU THINK YOU CAN GO AND FUCK SOME OTHER WOMAN ON OUR HONEYMOON, YOU BASTARD?!"

"Do what?! What are you talking about?! What woman?!" I screamed in disbelief at what was occurring.

"That FUCKING woman that you were all googly eyed over! You've been gone over an hour! I know you went to find her!"

"I fell asleep, Michelle! And I haven't been gone; you left me on the beach by myself!" I said, catching my breath.

"Yea right," she said kneeling down next to me which made me flinch. She grabbed at my trunks and pulled them down to my knees. "We'll see if you're telling the truth."

"What are you doing?!" I tried to fight her as I had no idea what she was capable of at this point and with my manhood staring back at me, there was no telling. She managed to get her face down between my legs and put my member into her mouth. I was totally confused as to what was going on and didn't know if I should be enjoying this or if I should be scared. As she began to get more into it, I felt my body betray me and start to relax. When she started moaning, I couldn't help but to fully let go and started thrusting into her mouth. It wasn't long before I released, which was unusual but I think with all the adrenaline that was surging through me, I couldn't hold back. As she sat up, she started to cry. In spite of what just happened, I hated to see my wife cry so I reached out for her and held her in my arms on the floor.

"I'm so sorry Gabe. I don't know what came over me. When you didn't come back in the room after me, all kinds of thoughts ran through my mind. I tried to call your cell but you left it here. And the longer you stayed out, the angrier I got. I started throwing stuff and threw your stuff out on the balcony. When I heard you come through the door, I still had the shoe in my hand and I just threw it. I'm so sorry baby. Please forgive me. I've ruined our honeymoon," she began to wail into my arms.

"Chellie, babe its ok. I would never do anything to hurt you, on our honeymoon or any other day. Why do you think I married you? I love you Michelle, no one else. You're all I need. Why would I mess that up for some floozy, that I didn't even see by the way," I said smiling at my wife. I couldn't deny the pain that still surged throughout my whole face but the euphoric state that she just put me in served as a small dose of Novocain.

"I love you too Gabe and you have brought so much to my life that I know I'll never be able to get from anywhere else. I have been trying to work on my anger and you know I have. I promise to go to counseling when we get back," she said sincerely before kissing me. I stood up and picked my wife up off of the floor and carried her into the bathroom where we showered and made love the way honeymooners were supposed to.

The first few months of being newly weds was perfect. We settled into our new home; spent countless hours decorating every room, lounged around naked, and christened every room with good old fashioned lovemaking. We even took another mini vacation to the Poconos Mountains. After the incident on our honeymoon, it seemed as though Michelle had done a complete 180 turn. She often times still got frustrated but instead of blowing up, she would just walk away. I was really beginning to see a transformation in my wife that I had been waiting nearly a year and a half to see. It seemed as if she really had awakened and realized the error in her ways and I couldn't have been any happier. She never did seek counseling but I didn't mind too much because she seemed to have been handling it very well on her own. It just seemed like each day I awoke to a new and more beautiful woman; what more could a guy ask for?

"Hey baby. Could you come here a minute?" I asked Chellie from the living room. When she walked into the room, I immediately got excited. It was something about Michelle's smile that always did me in. No matter what we were doing, all she had to do was smile and I would lose my cool completely.

"Yes baby," she said sitting next to me and kissing me on the lips.

"What do you say; I take you to that new spa downtown today?"

"REALLY?! Oh my goodness Gabe, the girls at work were raving about that spa!!" she squealed in my ear.

I laughed at her giddiness. "Well I mean, if you don't want to go, just say so," I teased.

"Stop! You know I want to go," she said, playfully pinching my arm. I grabbed her and held her down on the couch and planted a kiss gently on her lips. I looked into her eyes and wished we could be this way forever. No arguing, no attitudes, just bliss. I began planting light kisses on her neck and collarbone and then down to the top of her breasts. She started to rub my back and I knew that that meant she was getting turned on. One thing that has never lacked in our relationship was sexual chemistry. I returned to her lips and kissed her passionately. "Come on baby. Let's go before it gets too late," she said, breaking our embrace. She gently pushed me off of her and adjusted her top. I shook my head at my stupidity for recommending the spa to a woman BEFORE getting the opportunity to have sex.

"Alright babe. Let me just get washed up. Oh, before I forget, just wanted to let you know that I think I'm going to go hang out with Rick on Friday. He'll be in town and we haven't hung out since before the wedding," I said to her, kissing her on the neck, still trying my luck at maybe a quickie.

"What? But why? Friday nights are our movie nights," she said, erasing the smile from her face.

"Oh Chelles, don't be like that. We have every Friday night. Rick is only in town for two days and he's spending time with his family on Saturday."

"But why would he come on our day? For three months now you've never missed a Friday and now all of the sudden you want skip out?"

"Baby, please don't start this. Not now. Not while I'm still hard," I said pointing to the growing bulge in my pants.

"You think this is a joke Gabriel. I don't want you messing up our day!" she screamed, getting up with her hands on her hips.

"You know what, I see where this is going so I'm just going to go upstairs and get ready to leave," I said as I got up off the couch and walked out of the living room into the kitchen to head upstairs. Michelle followed right behind and I knew that she was not going to give in so easily this time.

"DON'T WALK AWAY FROM ME GABRIEL!" she screamed behind me.

I turned to face her and calmingly said, "Chellie, please calm down. Since you have off on Friday, we can spend the day together and then Rick and I can hang out that night. How's that? This way we all come out happy."

"Happy, huh? You wanna be happy?!" And in the blink of an eye, she had grabbed an unopened beer bottle that had been sitting on the counter amongst the rest of the groceries that she had not yet put away and swung it right into the side of my face. I screamed out in agony as blood ran down my face and I collapsed to the ground. "Don't think I don't know what you and Rick are trying to do! I know exactly what's going on!" she yelled at me as she took another bottle and smashed it into the back of my head. Before I blacked out I heard her yelling as she undid my pants, "If you think you are putting this dick in any other twat than mine, I promise you, I will cut it off!"

When I came to, I was still lying in the same spot on the floor and Michelle was sitting holding her knees to her chest, crying. When she saw me open my eyes, she crawled to me and helped me sit up. "Gabe, honey, I'm so sorry. I don't know what came over me. I screamed your name over and over and you just laid there. I thought you were dead. I thought I killed you. What is wrong with me?! I'm sorry Gabriel. Please forgive me," she rapidly stumbled over her words as the tears streamed down her eyes and landed on my hands that were holding me up on the floor. I reached up and touched the side of my face where she hit me first and it was bandaged with a gauge. Michelle was a nurse and kept first aid supplies all around the house so it was apparent that she patched me up during my blackout. Still stunned, I reached behind my head where she had bandaged the second impact spot. I honestly was at a lost for words and still very disoriented. She kept on pleading for my forgiveness but I couldn't muster up the strength to speak. I was in shock. I couldn't believe that I was here again and this time she almost killed me. How could a woman, whom I loved so much and saw so many wonderful things in, be so vicious? And for what? All because I wanted to spend time with my best friend? Is this what the next sixty something years of my life was going to be like? Walking on eggshells everyday just so that I won't tick her off? But I couldn't divorce her, I just simply didn't believe in that concept. When you get married, you take a vow of for better or for worse before God. God wouldn't bless a union that was not supposed to happen, would He? And how worse is worse? Was there anything worse than worse? Was this it? All of these questions raced through my mind as she continued to cry in my lap. I hadn't realized before that my pants were still undone until she reached into them and pulled me out. She started to kiss me there and my vision started to cloud. Every bone in my body wanted to push her away except the one in her mouth that refused to fight. The more she worked, the more I lost. When she finally finished, she cleaned me up and kissed me on the lips. She handed me a glass of water and two pills. "This should help with the pain," she said in a somber tone. She stared at me as I swallowed her recommended prescription. "Please say something to me Gabe," she begged.

Still sitting on the hard kitchen floor, I glared at her from half opened eyes and said, "You need help. I will no longer stay in this house until you get it."

She looked down at the floor for a few beats and said, "I understand. I promise I will go see a counselor but please don't leave me here by myself. Sleep in another room but just don't leave me. Please. Please don't leave me. Please," she begged as she began to cry into my shoulder.

"Fine. I'll stay in the guest room. But if you don't go to counseling, I will go and stay with my parents until you do," I said trying my best to get up while balancing on the lower cabinets. "I can't believe after only three months of marriage, we are here."

"I'll make it better baby. I swear," she said to me as I stumbled out of the kitchen and up the steps.

"Tell me, Mrs. Wise, what brings you here today?" Dr. Smith asked my wife. After several weeks of researching therapists, we came across Dr. Brenda Smith, an individual and marriage counselor who specialized in counseling and treatment for abusive women. I had yet to tell any of my family or friends about what was occurring behind our walls. To the outside world, we were the most loving couple and it had become like a job for me to ensure that it stayed that way. I just couldn't imagine what anyone would think of me as a man that I had been on the receiving end of my wife's hand. Not that abused women were any less strong but there's something about a man who is the victim in an abusive relationship that society undoubtedly brands as weak and therefore less of a man. I can't speak on any other situation but that was far from the case here. I was not a weak man. I was just a man who truly believed in the power of love and that no matter how many mistakes or faults a person has, it is your job to love them unconditionally, so who was I to look at my wife as if she's a monster? I will say one thing; however, monster or not, I was only human and I wasn't sure of how much will power I could continue to muster before I lost myself in the haunting thoughts that were starting to consume me.

Michelle cleared her throat before speaking. "We have been married now for almost five months and we need help," she said, letting her voice trail off.

"Ok. And what might that help be?" the doctor asked, obviously not letting my wife off that easily.

"We've been arguing and fighting a lot," she admitted. We both sat on opposite sides of the small couch and although she repeatedly glanced in my direction every few minutes, I kept my gaze locked to the floor as I listened as she continued to "we" her way through the conversation.

"Ok and how do these arguments and fights make you feel?"

My wife shrugged, "I don't know. No one enjoys fighting, I guess."

"I see," the doctor said, glancing over at me before scribbling something onto her notepad. "And exactly what have you been arguing about? Can you give me an example of a recent argument between the two of you?"

"I honestly can't remember. I just know that there was a lot of screaming going on and insults being thrown around."

"By whom, you or him," she asked, again glancing my way.

Michelle hesitated and glanced my way as well before responding, "I can't remember."

"That's alright, Michelle. That's why we're here. So that we can help you to remember and pin point the target problems within your marriage and move towards a realistic solution for the both of you," she assured. She wrote on her notepad for a few seconds before looking up and directly into my face. She addressed me, "Hello, Mr. Wise. You've been pretty quiet over there and you seem a tad withdrawn. What brings you here today?"

I finally lifted my head and stared at her straight on. I never understood why psychologists asked their patients dumb questions like that. She already knew why I was there; I told her when I made the appointment, why did she need me to repeat it. "My wife," was all I managed to say. I had always been a very cordial and warm man but for some reason being in that room, sitting on that couch in front of that woman made me infuriated. I just for the life of me couldn't understand how a positive and loving man such as me ended up in the marriage that we were sitting here dissecting. I couldn't get a hold on the unwillingness of my wife to admit her faults and responsibility in this whole situation. How she wanted to make it like WE had the issue when truth be told, before she came along, my life was as perfect as a living person could get.

"Your wife," she repeated. "Tell me, what about your wife?"

I looked over at my wife who immediately turned and looked away from me and then I stared back at the therapist and said, "So I guess we're all just going to sit here like a bunch of dumb asses as if we all don't know what the hell is going on here. My wife has severe anger problems and she has chosen to repeatedly take it out on my face!" I was surprised at my outburst but actually felt a bit relieved. I heard Michelle begin to sob next to me and for the first time since knowing her, did not care. "And please doc, don't insult my intelligence by asking me how that makes me feel. How would it make you feel to have the love of your life launch a beer bottle at your skull? As a matter of fact, I could show you and then later ask you how did that make you feel? How would you like that?" Michelle gasped when I said that. Being used to my mild mannerisms, she probably was more surprised at my sudden change in attitude than I was.

"I understand your frustrations, Mr. Wise but there is no need for idle threats. You all reached out to me for my assistance but I cannot help if neither of you are willing to cooperate. Help can only be rendered to those who are willing to receive it; otherwise it's just a bunch of useless jargon being tossed in the air for the wind to blow away. Now I think it best that I meet with each of you individually as well as a couple. I believe that each of you are holding back simply because of the other partner's presence. Each of you has some growth that needs to take place before the marriage can truly blossom. Because of the nature of your concerns, I strongly urge you two to temporarily separate until we progress through our counseling sessions. Now I know I am only your counselor and not the police, but I will say that violence of any kind towards anyone is not acceptable and I highly recommend the two of you not take this lightly. If you are serious about making a change towards the betterment of your individual and marital lives, I am here to assist you but it is YOU who will do the work. Now as I said, I would like to meet with each of you individually on a weekly basis and then monthly as a couple. So when's a good time for you two?"

"Mmm. This is delicious Gabe," my wife said to me as she put a forkful of the cucumber kimchi into her mouth. We were at one of our favorite Japanese restaurants, Tatu, in downtown Baltimore. Michelle and I were out celebrating her birthday. It had been almost four months since we both started therapy and five since we had spent significant time together, let alone, shared the same bed. Although immensely helpful, the therapy sessions were weighing heavy on us. There were many nights that she would come home exhausted from her session with the doctor and take it out on me. It seemed as though the abuse was getting worse rather than better. The doctor kept urging us to separate for the sake of our marriage and our individual safety but I just didn't want anyone asking any questions, so I just tried to keep my distance from Michelle on the nights she went to see Dr. Smith. I was learning a lot about myself as well; a lot of buried emotions and experiences that I guess I had blocked out of my memory. Dr. Smith said that she was beginning to see why my tolerance was so high for my wife. She said that because of some things that had occurred in my childhood, I had formed these ideals of what love was in my mind and therefore found it impossible to walk away, even if it hurt me to stay. No matter the hurt or trouble she put me through; I missed my wife terribly and had felt robbed of the expected newly wed bliss. We were coming up on our one year anniversary and yet with all of the turmoil that we were encountering, it felt like we had been married for forever. So in spite of all that was going on, I still decided that I would take her out for her birthday and try to make her feel special. Dr. Smith said it was important for me to express tenderness and compassion towards my wife during her moments of insecurity and I know she had been worried about whether I would acknowledge her on her birthday; so I decided to go all out for her on her day. I had a limo pick her up at home and had the driver drop her off at the spa that she and I never got the chance to go to. It had been opened for a few months now but neither she nor I had yet to venture over there so I thought it wonderful for her to experience it on her birthday. I purchase the largest package they had and left her to indulge completely for three hours. I then showed up with a new dress and shoes for her to wear to lunch at Tatu. For the first time in months, my wife smiled at me. It felt as if her smile had bandaged up everything that had been going on between us. We didn't kiss or even embrace but her smile was a welcomed start.

"I see. You're going to get full off of the salad alone," I said as she finished her third serving of the complimentary salad the waiter placed on our table.

"I know. I can't help it. I'm starved. I never knew how much relaxing made you hungry. Three hours in the spa really worked up my appetite."

"Well I'm glad you really enjoyed yourself, Chellie."

"Oh, I did Gabe. Thank you so much. This is by far the best birthday I've ever had," she said, smiling at me.

"Even better than last year? I did a great job last year. I'm hurt," I playfully said.

"Yes you did my love but I was so stressed out this time last year that I couldn't enjoy it. With the wedding being four months away, a birthday trip to DC was just a blur."

"Yea, you're right. We both were stressed. But I was just more so stressed because you were. I just wanted you to be happy," I said staring into her beautiful big eyes. "I still do." She stared at me for what seemed like forever before the tears started streaming down her face. She tried to shield her face so that none of the other restaurant patrons or wait staff would see her crying. I got up and came over to her side of the booth and put my arms around her and held my wife close. Feeling her warmth made me miss her even more; made me miss her touch, her kiss, and all those things good that we have not had in five months.

"I was going to take you on a boat cruise to Annapolis and check out some of the sites there but how about we get our food to go and head straight to the hotel suite that I got for us. What do you say? I miss you," I said, kissing her on her lips, "and I miss making love to you. I miss feeling you; feeling where I belong."

"Love making won't make our problems go away, Gabe," she said still crying. "I have a serious problem and I am ruining the best thing that has ever happened to me."

"I'm not looking for a quick fix. I am looking for my wife to allow me to love her. One day at a time. I love you Michelle. Yes, things have been strained between us but I believe in the power of love and I just need you to as well. Even if for one night, I want you to. No, I need you to let go and let me take care of you. Can you do that? Please? For me? For us?" I searched her eyes for a glimmer of hope and she searched mine for reassurance. After awhile, she nodded her head in agreement and kissed me passionately. I felt myself growing and knew that we needed to get going before I lost my cool and took her in the bathroom of this really nice restaurant and had my way with her up against the bathroom stall. As if reading my mind, the waiter came over to check on us and we informed him of our change of plans. From our position, I think the waiter caught on to what was going on and quickly boxed our food and had our check delivered promptly to the table.

I had reserved the Highlander Suite at the Renaissance Hotel just a few blocks away. I never claim to be rich but owning three successful gyms in the Baltimore and surrounding areas, I was able to provide a very comfortable life for my wife and I wanted to assure that she always had the best. I had the limo pick us up and drop us off at the hotel. I carried my wife from the lobby all the way to our room as people smiled at us, probably assuming that we were just the happiest couple they'd ever seen. Once inside the suite, I carried her straight to the separate bedroom and laid her on the soft down bed. I wanted to devour her right then and there but I knew that I had to take this slow and make this night last. I had room service stock the fridge with an assortment of fruits and a bottle of their finest champagne. For the remainder of the night, I pampered and catered to my wife in a way that no trained aesthetician or masseuse could. I would not go as far as to say that all of our problems were solved, but hearing her unforgettable moans in my ear made me feel like we were close.

The next morning, I ordered us breakfast in bed. We had been entangled in each other all night and I didn't want to move. I didn't even want to get out of the bed to answer the door when they delivered our food but Michelle playfully pushed me out of bed and I reluctantly obliged. We were having a great time and I was basking in her happiness. There was a calm over us that seemed almost eerie but considering what we had been going through, anything would seem strange at this point. We fed each other from the mounds of food that was piled high on the food cart. There was eggs, bacon, pancakes, bagels, fruit, yogurt, sliced potatoes, you name it. And we both feasted off of the entire thing. I guess a night full of love making will build up a couple's appetite. Not to mention the five month gap in absence from it. For the remainder of the day, we locked ourselves inside the suite and further explored our new heaven on earth. We made love in the shower, in the living room, on the solid oak dining room table, on the kitchen counter, and even in the floor to ceiling window overlooking the harbor. After our love sessions, we joked and laughed and conversed about our sessions with Dr. Mama, as we comically referred to Dr. Smith as because she had a way of making us feel like little kids being punished by their mothers although she was no more than ten years older than us. This was the first time that she and I discussed our sessions in any kind of manner, whether jokingly or not. And it surprised me at how easy it was. Michelle opened up about a lot of things that she discovered and I did the same. For the first time, I think I was able to effectively voice my concerns to my wife and she listened without getting defensive or hostile.

"What do you say we both stop doing our individual sessions?" Michelle said to me as we lay naked on the couch.

"How come? Thought you said that she was helping you to open your eyes to things?"

"Yes, exactly. And now that they are opened, I think we should just do couple's counseling and stop seeing the doctor one on one."

"Well, what did she say about it?"

"Oh, I haven't told her yet. But I'm sure she would agree. We both have made great strides. And now I think it best that we see her together, instead of alone."

"What are you scared of Chellie," I asked her sincerely.

"I'm not scared of anything, Gabriel," she snapped at me. I leaned in and kissed her softly on the lips to try and defuse the spark that was being lit in her. She took the bait and relaxed again.

"I'm not doubting your wishes baby, I'm just curious as to why the sudden change of mind."

"I just don't think that it'll continue to help us as a couple if you're being left alone for an hour with her," she said matter-of-factly.

"And what does that mean?" I asked, sitting up.

"It means that you are being left in a small room for an hour with a woman who you tell all your deep dark secrets to and that woman isn't me."

"But I'm not understanding what that has to do with anything, Chelles," I said, starting to feel a bit annoyed. "She's a therapist, that's what they get paid to do. Listen to people's deep dark secrets."

"It has everything to do with it. You're a gorgeous man in a vulnerable position and she's a divorced woman who hasn't gotten any in a very long time. You're like eye candy to her and I'm sure she's thirsty for more than that."

"Are you serious Michelle?! You're really saying this right now as we lay here naked together?!" I couldn't believe what I was hearing. Here we were having the best weekend in months and she had to go and drop this nuclear bomb. I got up and went to the window because I needed space and air from the toxins that were coming from her.

"I just don't trust her around you. I'm sure she's telling you all kinds of outlandish things."

"You have got to be kidding me! You can not be doing this right now. And how did you even know that she was divorced?" I asked her over my shoulder.

"Why does it matter? And why are you upset? I would think that you would be ok with it as you didn't even want to see her one on one in the first place."

"I didn't at first but now I do. She has really helped me out a lot and I'm upset because I can't believe that all you can think about is whether or not she will try to seduce me!"

"I see the way she looks at you now. It's different. She dresses differently and everything. And I know I'm not being paranoid like I normally am. She's even started dealing with me differently. Tell me I'm wrong," she challenged.

I just stood there staring out the window for a few moments in disbelief.

"Gabe? Tell me I'm wrong," she repeated, a little more stern. "Tell me she hasn't changed. Tell me that I have nothing to worry about with you two." When I still didn't respond she paused for a few minutes and then asked, "Is there something I should know, Gabe? Gabriel?! Do you hear me?!"

"Something like what, Michelle?" I turned and looked at her. "Something like, I've been sleeping with our therapist? Huh? Is that what you want to hear? That she gives me what my own wife won't. That she fills a void that my wife of eight months has yet to be able to fill and that I'm not so sure she ever will. Huh? That the very couch you've laid your head on week after week had her juices all over it just the day prior. That she's able to take me all into her mouth until I completely disappear without a trace. Is that what you want me to say?!" My heart was pounding so hard through my chest that you could visibly see it. Michelle just sat there with her mouth hanging open with a look that I understood so clearly. Rage. It was the same look my biological mother gave my father right before she stabbed him in the heart after he had revealed his adulterous activities to her. I couldn't believe how I had managed to duplicate my parents' marriage. I was five when my father died at the hands of that deranged woman. I was adopted by the Wise family soon after my mother was committed to the mental institution and they had raised me in a very loving and stable household. Although I was aware that they were not my real parents, I had somehow managed to block out everything that happened before they came along and sort of started my life from them on out. But my sessions with Dr. Smith unlocked those hidden demons and I began to see my life and how I got to where I was more clearly.

While in a session one day, I revealed to her about the time when I was four and my biological mother chained me to a beam in our basement and left me there for four days all because I wet the bed. I became extremely emotional and enraged and started throwing things around her office. When she tried to calm me down, I kissed her. It wasn't intentional at first but then she kissed me back and the rest is, well you know. I loved my wife with all of my might and never wanted to hurt her but Brenda was my release. I had a lot of anger built up and stored inside of me and I took it out on her and she didn't mind one bit because the rougher I was, the harder she came. I felt horrible at first about it but the more Michelle fought me, the more I fucked Brenda. But this weekend made me feel like things were well between my wife and I; like we actually might be onto some change, so when she brought up not seeing the doctor individually, I became enraged. I didn't care anymore. I was sick of this marriage. I was sick of my life. I was sick of trying to be a good man to the women in my life and always falling short. I couldn't take it anymore. I couldn't take her abuse, her insecurities, her yelling, name calling, none of it. All I ever wanted was a life of normalcy and staring into this woman's eyes in front of me, I just knew that I would never get it. I tried to calm my mind and heart beat down by walking into the bedroom but before I took a step, Michelle leaped off of the couch and slapped me hard across the face.

"YOU MOTHERFUCKER! You have been fucking her! I knew it! I knew it! I hate you! I hate you!" she screamed as she repeatedly punched and kicked at me as I tried to hold her back. She kicked me in between my legs and it sent the most excruciating pain up my spine. All the anger that I had ever held inside towards her and towards my mother seemed to crawl up my back and out to my hands. I felt as though I was no longer myself but another man in another time. I reached out for her neck and gripped tightly. She started to swing wildly at me but I didn't let go. She was screaming and kicking but oddly enough, I couldn't hear anything. It was like I was in a tunnel and all I could see were her eyes. This time it wasn't rage, it was death. Her kicks began to lessen and her punches were sporadic. Her face started to turn a slight purple and I knew that if I let go now, she may have a chance to survive; so I held on tighter. I wanted her to feel the pain, the misery, the death that I had felt for twenty nine years. I wanted her to feel the agony that sat buried inside of me; the pain that she had caused to resurface. As her body fell limp, I released her and let her fall to the floor. I stood there for awhile watching her lifeless body. Strangely, she lay in the same position that my father did when my mother pulled the knife out of him. So I guess my life had come full circle. They say the way you come into this earth will be the way you go out. Since this prophesy had seem to come to pass, I took a deep breath and walked over to my cell phone. As I dialed 911, I contemplated as to whether I should call my therapist.

Baggage is a Disease

"Morning gorgeous," he said to me as my eyes reluctantly fluttered open.

"Morning handsome," I growled back in my groggy morning voice.

"Man, I didn't know I was sleeping next to Darth Vader!" He joked. I playfully punched him and we began to wrestle with each other in bed. Sam and I had been dating for eight months and there was never a dull moment between us. Even how we met was exciting.

I was walking through Midtown one day when this guy snatched my purse right out of my hand. Being the Brooklyn raised girl that I am, I wasn't about to let some punk just come and violate me like that so I ran after the fool. I'm screaming and hollering for him to stop but he either ran track or was just used to running from cops because he was speeding down the street, bumping and pushing people out of his way. And of course that would be the day that I wore my highest of heels and tightest of dresses, so my agility was limited. About a minute into my pursuit of him, one of my heels gave way and I went flying face first onto the hard concrete sidewalk. And true to the New Yorker form, most people kept on about their business, too busy to care about some clumsy girl laid out on the ground. And as if I weren't mortified enough, the most gorgeous man I'd ever laid eyes on approached me and asked if I were alright. Unable to speak, I just shook my head no. He extended his hand to me and helped me up off the ground. When he asked me what happened, I told him some idiot had just snatched my purse and that I tried to play hero and go after him. He asked me to describe the guy the best I could and the direction I saw him run. When I did, he went high tailing down the street in the direction I pointed out. A bit confused, I screamed after him but he was gone. I stood there for a few minutes totally unsure of what to do next. I flagged a police car down and explained the absurd events to the two police officers. After a few moments, I heard a guy screaming profanities and threats from behind me; loud enough to almost drown out the loud Midtown noise. I turned and saw my knight in shining armor approaching me and the cops with a handcuffed guy in one hand and my purse in the other. I stood there in disbelief that he had actually captured the perp who had just run off with my bag. Come to find out the idiot was high on drugs and had dumped the contents of my purse out a few blocks down and was searching for money out in the open in broad daylight when my rescuer reached him. My knight introduced himself to me as Samuel Banks, an off duty police officer for New York City; and the rest has become history in the making. Being from Flatbush, Brooklyn, I have had my share of womanizers, assholes, players and pimps; so being around Sam was intriguing to me because he was totally not what I was used to. Being raised by both of his parents in the suburbs of Virginia, Sam was a wholesome southern man who knew how to treat a woman. He's thirty one with no children, owns his own house, has very little debt, and is polite and chivalrous. Above all of that though, he had managed to do something that no man that I'd ever encountered had; he made me laugh. And I don't mean a light chuckle; I'm talking a strong belly laugh that makes you feel like you've just gone through an intense ab workout. To some that may sound trivial but being from such hard beginnings, that ability meant the world to me. I know that they say no one is perfect but Sam was probably as close as one would ever get to it. I was almost ashamed to bring him around my neighborhood. But I wanted him to know that even though this was where I lived, it did not define me. Well, not anymore. And true to his wonderful spirit, he embraced my situation and didn't allow my address to compromise what we were building together. He even befriended some of the guys in my building and had them on "watch out" for me when he was not around. Even though they were street boys and he was a cop, they respected him because he respected me. As a kid, I never heard stories of fairy tales and happy endings but each day Sam and I continued to create our own magical Disney adventure.

"Stop Sam! No fair! You're stronger than me!" I playfully screamed under him as he performed one of his wrestling moves that had my whole body in a pretzel.

"Be quiet and take it like a man!" he laughed, applying more weight onto me.

"OWW baby, serious. You're hurting me," I whined.

He jumped up and said, "I'm sorry, Trish. Are you ok?"

"Sike!" I said as I jumped on top of him and tried to pin him down. He started tickling me until I fell over laughing. He got on top of me but instead of pinning me down again, he kissed me softly on the lips. Without a word being said, I knew that was his way of saying playtime was over and that adult time was about to begin. Waking up to a playful romp followed by great sex was something I could come to live with. I guess this story was a little too grown up for the Disney crowd after all.

"Hey baby, how's your day going?" I crooned into the phone.

"Better now that I'm talking to you," Sam responded back.

"Look at you. Well thank you baby. That makes me feel good."

"Then my job is done. How are you today, gorgeous?"

"I'm ok. I had to fire the girl I was telling you about last night; the one who was late every day. I've just given her too many warnings and we're doing inventory today and even the people who weren't scheduled to work today had to be here on time. So I just couldn't let her slide anymore. I just hate having to take someone's job away from them though."

"But you had to do what you had to do baby. You are the store manager now and you have to lay down the law. You've worked hard to get where you are and the people who work under you are a reflection of you and your work. Don't let some irresponsible girl come in and make you look bad. You're too new in the game to let that happen," Sam assured me.

"Thank you Sam. I needed that. I don't want to be the mean boss but I'm no push over either. Shit, I'm from Flatbush!" I laughed.

"Damn right. You better tell those bitches who you are baby!"

"You silly, boy."

"I'm just glad I can put a smile on your face babe. I don't like to see or hear you down for any reason."

"And that's why I love you. But look, I'm about to head back to work, my break is almost over."

"Ok gorgeous, but one more thing. The reason I called you is because it's my mother's birthday next weekend and I know that's your weekend off, so I wanted to know if you wanted to come with me to Virginia to meet my parents and attend her fiftieth birthday celebration."

In the eight months that we'd been dating, we had yet to meet each other's families. I didn't have much family and the ones that were around were either in jail or strung out on drugs; including my mother, whom I hadn't seen in almost a year. I had no idea where she was or if she was even alive. The last time I saw her, she was tricking for a hit. I tried numerous times to get my mother into a rehab program but she would always leave before she finished. I had an older brother who was doing 4 consecutive life sentences for murdering a family out in Staten Island over a drug deal gone terribly wrong. And as far as my daddy; well, rumor had it, he was the pimp that was tricking my mother out all those years but no one knows for sure; not even my mother. I was mainly raised by my grandmother who passed away when I was seventeen so needless to say, there isn't much family for Samuel to meet. I hadn't told him everything about my family and childhood but he knew it wasn't pretty and that I had worked really hard to make a change in my life. His family on the other hand, seemed to be the Huxtables reincarnated. His three sisters were younger than him and amazingly they all had the same parents, whom as I'd mentioned before were still married. Even both of his sets of grandparents were still married to their first spouse. I had no idea that still existed, especially in the African American community. I had spoken to his mother on the phone numerous times and I couldn't help but feel a twinge of jealousy as I wished I were lucky enough to have a loving person like her caring after me. His family, at least from my point of view, seemed to be the epitome of what a real family should be. All of them were still in Virginia and Sam's crazy work schedule kept him from being able to visit them as often as he'd like, so I knew he was ecstatic about being able to take the weekend off to visit them. I was even more ecstatic and honored that he was asking me to join him. I was sure this was a big deal to him to bring a woman home to his family as he had made it clear that he had always been very picky of the women he introduced to his family. I couldn't help but to think that maybe this was going to be a major turning point in our relationship. We had already voiced our love for one another but this was way more concrete than that. This was as if he were now presenting me to the board of officials for the final seal of approval in order to go forward in our relationship. What would happen if they accepted me and loved me as he has? Would we start planning for a future together? But what if they didn't? What if they hated me and called me a ghetto hood rat? Would their opinion matter so much to him that he dump me?

"Trisha? Are you still there?" he asked, interrupting my thoughts before they became too manic.

"Yes, Sam. Sorry."

"Well did you hear me, babe?"

"No I didn't, sorry boo. I got distracted," I lied to save myself from seeming silly. "What did you say?"

"I asked if you would like to come with me next weekend to meet my family and celebrate my mother's fiftieth birthday," he repeated.

"Sure, I would love to Sam!" I said in fake surprise.

"Good. Well get back to work, gorgeous and I'll see you later on tonight when I get off of work."

"Thank you boo. And thank you for inviting me to go with you next weekend. I know how much your family means to you."

"That's because you're my woman and you mean almost just as much as they do and it's about time that you all got acquainted. You never know, you all might be seeing more of each other for years to come," he said and I could hear the smile in his voice.

I smiled for the rest of the day. I didn't even care anymore that I had one less person helping out at the store; my Disney story had me on cloud nine.

The whole ride to Virginia, I was a nervous wreck. I had never met a man's family before; especially a man like Sam. Things like that didn't happen where I was from. You're lucky if you get to even meet his mama. The entire seven hour ride, Sam kept asking if I were alright and of course I kept nodding and smiling, saying that I was. He tried to reassure me that they would love me and I had nothing to worry about but I knew that he didn't know for sure so his words fell on deaf ears. Once we pulled up to his parents' house; the house with the three car garage overlooking the lake, I knew I definitely had my work cut out for me. The two story house looked like those houses in Long Island they showcase on the Sunday morning real estate channel. As we pulled into the driveway, a woman appeared in the doorway with a grin that spread from ear to ear. She stepped out onto the porch and all the anxiety that I had been feeling, doubled.

"Relax baby. She'll love you. I promise," Sam said, reaching over and grabbing my hand.

"I'm relaxed baby. Just a little tired, that's all," I lied.

"Well, let's go so you can lie down," he said as he climbed out of the car and came around the passenger side to open my door.

"There's my favorite son," his mother beamed as we approached her on the porch.

"I'm your only son, mama," he laughed as they embraced.

"All the more reason for you to be my favorite one now isn't it?"

"Very funny. Mama, this is Trisha. Trisha, this is the first love of my life, my mother Irene."

"Very nice to finally put a face to a name and voice Trisha," his mother sweetly said as we shook hands.

"The pleasure is all mines. Thank you for allowing me to celebrate with you and your family."

"No worries. Samuel speaks very highly of you so any love of my Sammy is already a part of the family in my book," she said as she reached out and hugged me. I wondered how much he told her about me. I hoped not too much. I didn't want her thinking of me as a reformed hoodrat. I wanted to have a blank slate with his family. Reputations are hard to live up to; especially when you're not trying to.

"My mother still insists on calling me Sammy like I'm five years old."

"Oh hush chile. You'll always be my Sammy. Now you two get on in there and eat. I made ya'll some lunch cause I knew that you'd be hungry from your drive in," she said as she escorted us into the house. Just as I suspected; the house was gorgeous on the inside too. Very well kept and tidy. The split level home smelled of lavender and vanilla. The second level opened out over the foyer and the lower level was tucked quietly away below us.

"We already ate mama and Trisha is a bit tired so I was just going to nap with her and then get up later and eat," Sam said as he carried our luggage up the short staircase to the second level.

"Oh, ok. I see," she said a bit disappointed. "Well, you two are in the guest room downstairs. There are fresh towels and washcloths folded on the bed and I changed the linen before you arrived. Dinner will be ready around seven." And with that, she turned and walked into the kitchen.

Once we were downstairs in the guest room out of ear shot, I said, "Is she alright? I hope we didn't offend her."

"Don't worry about her. My mother is a big baby when it comes to me. She smothers me every time I'm around. She's a little in her feelings right now but she'll get over it. Trust me, don't worry," he said as he put his arms around my waist and pulled me into his chest. "Now, I've just driven seven hours sitting next to the most beautiful and sexy woman I know. All I want to do right now is feel her body next to mine; not talk about my mama," he said as he kissed from my neck to the top of my breasts.

"Sam, stop. Not in your parents' house," I protested weakly.

"Come on baby, why you think they put us down here," he said, still making his way down my body with his kisses. "Speaking of down," he said as he lifted my dress and got up close and personal with my pleasure spot.

"Sam," was all I could muster the strength to whisper as I collapsed onto the bed.

"Hello sleepy heads," his mother greeted us as Sam and I walked into the kitchen together. After passing out from our lovemaking, we both took a needed nap and were awaken by the smells of home cooking and laughter upstairs. Reluctantly we both rose and showered and decided it best to join the masses for dinner.

"Hey mama. Ya'll started without us?" Sam asked, sounding very disappointed.

"Of course not. I was just about to come and wake you all," his mother said as she continued to set the table.

"And who might this be?" An older gentleman asked as he handed Sam's mother a bowl of potato salad for her to place on the table.

"Pop, this is Trish. Trish, this is my father, James."

"Nice to meet you," I said to his father as I extended my hand.

"Pleasure is all mine miss lady," he said as he took my hand in his and planted a feather kiss on the back of it.

"And I'm Angel, his baby sister," she said, jumping up to take my hand from her father's grasp.

"Nice to meet you Angel."

"I'm so sure," she said as she eyed me up and down. "So I hear you've only known my brother for a short period of time. How'd you manage to pull off meeting the family that fast?"

"Excuse my sister," Sam interjected. "She was dropped on her head as a baby and has never seemed to recover," he said, playfully grabbing her into a headlock.

"Stop idiot! You mess my weave up and you're going to give me the three hundred bucks to get it fixed!" she snapped as she pushed him off her.

"Alright you two. Please, don't start with each other already. Your brother hasn't even been here for all of twenty four hours yet and you're starting already, Angel," his mother said. She turned to me and said, "Trish, I apologize for my daughter's rudeness. I assure you she has been properly home trained, she just doesn't apply any of it. Although he's the oldest, Angel thinks she's Sam's protector."

"That's cause she loves me," Sam said in a baby voice, grabbing his baby sister and planting kisses all over her face.

"Ahh, come on Sam, stop!" she yelled but didn't push him away.

"Hello, I'm Mona and this is Kim. We're his other sisters. You really have to excuse my family. They're all a little special," she laughed as I shook her and her other sister's hands.

"It's alright. I think it's nice that you guys get along so well. I've heard so much about you guys and it's nice to finally meet you all," I smiled.

"Well, everything is all set. Let's eat!" Sam's father said.

By the end of dinner, my face was sore from laughing so hard at the antics of his family. From Angel's financial and men problems to Sam's father's many failed attempts at being a homemade handyman. There was a brief period of anxiety when the women of his family sent me through the inevitable question and answer session; especially when asked about my family. I tried to glorify it as much as the truth would allow me to. Other than a few snide remarks from Angel, they actually understood and seemed to relax a little more. His mother even reached out from across the table and caressed my hand when I admitted that I had no idea about my mother's whereabouts. When the mood seemed to turn somber, Sam came to the rescue by suggesting we play board games. I thought that was kind of cheesy and was about to comment when Kim and Angel jumped up and ran to go get some games. Truth be told, I had never played board games and thought that was something that white families did. But then again, I was hanging with the Huxtables. To my surprise, I had never had more fun. After killing it in "Monopoly" and "Sorry", I was hooked. Before we knew it, it was almost midnight.

"Goodness, look at the time. We sitting around here like we have nothing to do tomorrow," his mother said, as she started gathering all the paraphernalia.

"Mama, relax, relax," Sam protested as he tried to stop her from cleaning. "This is your weekend. You and pop can go on to bed and we'll clean up out here."

"Who's we?" Angel questioned with her hand on her hip.

"All of her beautiful children, Angelica; whom she has spent the last thirty two years nurturing and caring for. One of which she is STILL doing the aforementioned for," Sam threw back.

"Oh, it's like that. Ok, I get it. I see what this is," she continued to huff as she walked into the kitchen and turned on the faucet to start the dishes.

"Mama, I still think they made a mistake in the hospital. You sure they didn't switch her?" Sam joked as he kissed his parents goodnight.

"Behave. Don't talk about my baby like that," his mother said as she escorted her husband out of the living room.

"Night," Sam and his two sisters said in unison.

"Goodnight," his parents responded back.

When we had the house back in order, Kim and Mona said their goodnights and went to bed. Angel never reappeared after finishing the dishes.

"I hope they weren't too much for you," Sam said as he massaged my feet as we sat down on the couch.

"No, not at all. Your family is great," I sincerely said.

"Even Angel?"

"Even Angel," I laughed.

"I guess I should have warned you about her. I was eleven when she was born and was very protective of her. It was something about her. She was different from Kim and Mona. Mona is very independent; always has been. And Kim keeps to herself. Those two didn't need much attention; they could fend for themselves early on. Angel was the kind of baby that knew how to get and keep the attention of everybody. She would cry just to keep your focus. If you stopped paying her attention to talk to someone or do something, she would cry and wouldn't stop until you turned your attention back to her. It was like she was always unsure about her importance and constantly needed reminding. And it was like I was in tuned to that, so I've always been the one to cater to that. I don't know why, but she and I have always been close like that. So whenever I have a girlfriend, she gets jealous because she knows that my attention is being diverted. But she's harmless. You are the first girl I've brought home in years, so she knows that it's serious. She's just going to give you a hard time just to make sure you're here to stay which I already know you are so you have nothing to worry about."

His last comment jolted me and I suddenly became uneasy. So much so that I unknowingly pulled my foot away from his grasp.

"What's wrong, babe?" he asked.

"Nothing. Sorry, think it's just a cramp," I lied. Why was I lying? And why did that comment; "*you're here to stay*", make my stomach do flips? And not in a good way. That's what every girl wants to hear from the man they love, right? I suddenly started feeling sick to my stomach. "Let's go lay down. I suddenly don't feel too well."

For the first time in our relationship, I slept on the far end of the bed that night. Every time he reached out for me, I pulled away and complained about cramps. It seemed like the trip had caused Sam to open up more about his feelings and intentions with me and honestly, it was starting to scare me. It's one thing to want something but it's a completely other thing to actually have it. Could I really settle down with this man? Would he really accept all of me? There was still so much that we didn't know about each other; more so, that he didn't know about me. How can he be so sure that he will continue to want me around years from now? My questions put me into a deep sleep and somewhere in the middle of the night, I found myself cuddled in his arms. This couldn't be wrong.

The next day was hectic. We were running last minute errands for Sam's mother's party that night. His family seemed to take to me very well, even Angel. I even ran out with his sisters to pick up his mother's cake and we laughed and joked the whole time. They told me embarrassing stories about Sam from their childhood and filled me in on their own embarrassing moments. By the time we reached the hall where the party was being held, we all had exchanged numbers and Facebook info.

"Looks like things went well," Sam said to me as we met him at the entrance.

"Good choice, bro," Mona said as she winked at her brother before escorting her sisters inside.

"Wow. What did you do? Even Angel is smiling," he said grabbing me into a tight embrace.

"I didn't do anything. I was just myself," I said as I kissed him lightly on the lips.

"Yes and that's why I told you that you had nothing to worry about because they would see what I do and probably love you more. Not sure that's possible though," he said as he kissed me back more intense.

"You're a wonderful man, you know that? How did I get so lucky?" I said, staring into his eyes. Maybe this was possible. Maybe I could really be with him and open up fully and just give him all of me.

"It's in my genes," he teased as he playfully smacked me on my butt.

We walked into the hall and a lot of his family had already shown up. There was a DJ playing oldies but goodies and everyone was talking and laughing with one another. We walked around and Sam introduced me to everyone. Everyone seemed to take to me as well; I even danced with one of his great uncles on the dance floor. They showed a slide show of his mother throughout the years and I must say that the woman was gorgeous. She got choked up as she gave her thank you speech for all of her family and friends coming out to support her on her birthday. They opened the floor for people to say some words to her. A few of her brothers and sisters got up and talked about her and of course her husband had everyone in tears as he admitted that he could not live without his wife by his side. Sam's sisters all got up and said some wonderful words to their mother. When it was Sam's turn at the mic, he looked obviously nervous. He had a worried look on his face as if he had stage fright. After clearing his throat about five times he began his speech.

"Anyone who knows me, knows that Irene Margaret Banks has been the love of my life, for all of my life," he began as he cleared his throat one more time. "She has displayed what a real woman should be like. The characteristics and the mannerisms of a virtuous woman. My sisters always tease me about not ever bringing a girl home to meet my parents; well, to meet my mom because I knew pops would like her as long as she was pretty." The room burst into laughter and his dad nodded in agreement. "But Irene held herself and her children in a higher regard than that. Sorry pops. She made sure that she always exemplified a strong, loving, tender yet firm wife and mother. Whenever my parents had a disagreement, she would always make sure that none of us were around to witness those bad times that every couple goes through. And if it got really bad, she would sit us down and talk to us about it. She was the kind of mother that would beat you for doing something wrong and then rock you to sleep afterwards. She was and still is the toughest gentle person on earth and her heart is as pure as they come. So whenever I would meet a girl and decide to date her, I would ask if she were 'Irene-Ready'." Another round of laughter erupted. "And the answer was always no. The girls met my standards but they never met the 'Irene-Ready' standards. Until now. Eight months ago I was blessed enough to literally stumble upon a very beautiful woman who changed my life."

I sat next to Sam wide eyed as I couldn't believe what he was beginning to say. I started looking around the room as everyone's faces equally matched my shocked looked; everyone that is except his mother's, who had the biggest grin on her face. As he continued on about how he and I met and how every day is a new adventure, I started to feel like I wanted to throw up. Why was he doing this? Why was he putting our relationship out there for everyone? I mean, granted they knew that we were together but why did they have to know the details of his feelings towards me.

"Now I know some of you are like, 'why is this fool taking up his mother's time to talk about some girl?' Well because this girl is definitely 'Irene-Ready' and she has been given the stamp of approval by Mrs. Banks herself. And I figured what better time than now, in front of my entire family," he said as he turned to me and reached for my hand which by then was shaking profusely and knelt in front of me, "to say to you Trisha, I love you with every fiber in my being and I know that we've got so far to go but once you know you just know. And what I know is that if you'll allow me to, I would love to start a life together. Will you marry me?" he ended as he pulled out a square box and revealed a huge rock in the center of it. The vomiting feeling was getting worse and worse by the second until I felt it rushing up my throat and into my mouth. I tried to hold it in but it was hitting violently and it all came rushing out and onto Sam's shirt and pants. I jumped up and ran out the hall and into the fresh night air. I heard a lot of commotion behind me as I ran out as I'm sure people had their own conclusions as to what was going on.

"Trisha baby, what's wrong?" Sam screamed after me as he reached the outside area.

"Is she alright?" Kim said from behind me. I was bent over trying to catch my breath.

"Trisha honey, are you alright baby," Sam's mother said next to me.

"She's probably pregnant. That's why he's asking her to marry him," I recognized Angel's voice not too far away.

"Angel, go back inside," his mother demanded.

"I'm just saying. Eight months isn't a long enough time. It's gotta be something," she said as her voice disappeared.

"I'm sorry Sam," I said, still bent over.

"No baby, it's ok. I know it's a lot that I just threw your way and I'm sorry I did it in this fashion but,"

"No, it's not that. I'm sorry, I can't marry you."

"Oh... Hey, guys can you give us a few minutes alone please?" he said to everyone behind us.

As I stood up, I saw that there was a large crowd behind me and I was glad that he dismissed them all because what I was about to say, I didn't want him to find out in front of fifty other people.

"I'm sorry if I'm going too fast. We can take as long as you like," he started

"It's not the speed," I said as I stood up straight and looked him square in the eyes and saw the concern on his face.

"Well what is it? Is it someone else? Are you having doubts about us? You're not pregnant are you cause we've been using protection, although I know anything is possible" he spit questions out at me that made me feel queasy again.

"No, no, there's no one else and I'm not pregnant."

"So what is it? Why am I covered in vomit? Do you not love me anymore? You've been kind of distant since we got here." He was talking so fast that my head started spinning. I needed space, time to think and he wasn't allowing me that privilege and it was making me angry. "What is it Trisha? Tell me."

I closed my eyes but his questions didn't stop. "I'M HIV POSITIVE DAMMIT!" I screamed. When I opened my eyes, his mouth was open but no words were coming out. I heard a gasp behind me and saw his mother standing there with the same look on her face.

"You're fucking kidding me, right? Please woman, tell me you are just kidding!" he said almost begging.

"I'm sorry Samuel. I wish I were," I said with my chin to my chest.

"You mean you have AIDS?!" he screamed.

"No, I don't have AIDS, I'm HIV positive. There's a difference," I defended.

"Is there?! I've been kissing and sexing you for eight months and not once did you think to tell me some shit like this?!" he screamed in my face.

"Of course I did! I wanted to tell you the very first time we went out but how do you tell someone that?" I said with tears in my eyes.

"EASY! Like this, Hey my name is Trisha and I'm a nasty bitch with HIV!"

"Ok now son, that's enough. Let's go inside and cool off," his mother said, putting her arms around his shoulders.

"I'm good ma; I'm not going back inside. I'm going home," he said as he walked towards his car. He stopped and turned back towards me and said, "And to think that I really thought you were the one. This whole time your nasty ass was just out to get me caught up in your shit. You need to go back to that slum that you came from and find the nigga that gave you that shit or that you gave it to or whatever and suck on his dick some more cause I'm through with your dirty ass. And you better pray to Jesus, Allah, Buddha, and the motherfucking Pope that I don't have that shit cause if I do, I WILL go to jail for murder! You can find your own damn way back to New York, bitch!" he said as he turned and walked out of site.

All I could do was stand there with tears flowing down my eyes. "I was raped," I said to the air through tears.

Made in the USA
Charleston, SC
11 May 2012